DP
6/15

Murder of Crows

The Twenty-Sided Sorceress: Book Two

Annie Bellet

Cover designed by Ravven (www.ravven.com)
Formatting by Polgarus Studio (www.polgarusstudio.com)
First edition, 2014

If you want to be notified when Annie Bellet's next novel is released and get free stories and occasional other goodies, please sign up for her mailing list by going to: http://tinyurl.com/anniebellet. Your email address will never be shared and you can unsubscribe at any time.

This book is dedicated to Matt, Greg, and Jane,
for putting up with me.
And also to the Indie Asylum, for keeping me sane.

The battlefield was quiet in the summer sunlight. I heard only the hum of insects and a light shushing of wind. My back was sweaty where I pressed it against the bark of an oak, using the tree as cover from the enemy I couldn't see or hear, but knew was out there across the meadow. The pile of ammo at my feet had dwindled down to a double handful. In the shade of the trees to my right, Harper's brother Max lay prone, red dripping down his chest and staining the dead leaves beneath him.

To the other side of me, Alek crouched among slender aspen trees, his arm useless, his leg oozing colors, his gun on the ground. He gave me a Gallic shrug and slight smile, the afternoon breeze lifting his white blond hair off his forehead, his ice blue eyes glinting with dark humor.

A paintball burst on a tree trunk just over his head.

"So," he said. "We're out manned and out gunned."

"Maybe you should untie my hands," I said.

"That's not the point of the game," Max pointed out.

"For a corpse, you are doing a lot of talking." I glared at the kid, but he just grinned.

Peeking around the tree, I surveyed the meadow. Ezee's body was a dark lump in the grass. He was the only one I'd brought down so far, no thanks to the "help" on my team. I was pretty damn sure Alek and Max had gotten shot on purpose so that I'd have to figure out how to take down Harper and Ezee's twin, Levi, on my own.

We were gathered on this lovely summer Sunday out at The Henhouse Bed and Breakfast where Harper and Max's mother Rosie was letting us train. Three months ago, I'd saved her from an evil warlock, but exposed myself to an old rival. A man who would come after me.

Kind of surprising he hadn't already, really. Samir, my psychokiller ex, had restrained himself to sending cryptic postcards and had yet to show his face. I knew he would tire of sending messages and show up eventually.

I needed to get my sorceress powers stronger before that happened. Much, much stronger.

Hence the paintball game of ultimate unfairness. Ezee, Harper, and Levi were all accomplished paintballers as well as shape shifters, which meant they got super speed, strength, extraordinary senses, and great reaction time to go with their crack shot abilities, and they were on the opposing side. That left me with Alek, who should have been good at paintball since he could shoot real guns just fine, and Max, who was more enthusiastic than skilled. Sure, my team were shifters also, and yet here they were, out of the game already without more than a couple shots fired.

Leaving me, with my hands literally tied behind my back, to somehow win this thing. Magically. No gun. No hands. Just power. Only the rules said I had to win by hitting my opponents with paintballs, so I couldn't just wrap a shield around myself and go hunt them down that way. No shields allowed today, either.

They'd taken away all my fun. By "fun" I do mean crutches. Bastards.

A green ball splattered on the tree trunk behind me.

"Best two out of three?" I yelled.

Another paintball, this one orange, smacked into the tree, misting paint onto my nose.

"Guess that's a no," I muttered as I wiped my nose on my shoulder as best I could.

"Perhaps if you sit here all day, they will get bored and come to you," Alek said. He pulled a knife from his boot, using its point to pick at his fingernails.

I considered telling him where to stick that knife but decided to concentrate on how I was going to win this thing. I looked around the tree again. The meadow sloped slightly downhill toward the thicket of saplings and brush where Harper and Levi were holed up. They couldn't cross the meadow, as Ezee's suspiciously snoring body demonstrated, but neither could I go to them. I couldn't even see them down there and I knew they'd be able to see me much clearer with their supernaturally enhanced senses.

If only my spirit guardian, the somewhat wolf-like creature I creatively called Wolf, was useful for this shit. She was lounging in the shade deeper into the trees in which I was currently hiding, her tufted ears perked as I glared at her and she swished her long and thick black tail. Wolf could only help me with magical attacks and problems. Not that she would help here anyway. She seemed to understand this was all play and was content to watch. Traitor.

I twisted my arms a bit, testing the orange baling twine's knots. They weren't tied that tight, the purpose wasn't to really restrain me but to keep me from using gestures to help me cast spells. I was much better at casting when I could use my hands to direct energy. It was another crutch. Truly great magic shouldn't need hands. I needed my brain to be able to think outside the normal physical limitations of the world.

It's easy to pick up a couple rocks or paintballs with magic when you can just extend it as a gesture your body and mind are already used to. But visualizing having three or four or five hands? Tougher. The human brain isn't used to being able to lift five things at once in all directions. In order to get my brain to do it, I had to break reality a little, starting in my thoughts.

Break reality. I clung to that thought. I had been flinging paintballs at them like I was the gun, but there was really no need to do so. I didn't need to conform to the physics of a gun when I threw. I could be like that one cheesy movie where they bent bullets and stuff.

Theoretically.

"You aren't dead," I whispered to Alek, "so get ready to help." I didn't have super senses, but I had someone who did.

Alek's leg and arm had been hit, but he wasn't technically out, though he couldn't shoot anymore. That was okay, I didn't need his gun. I needed the tiger in him, his keen hunter's senses and instincts. He was a freakin' Justice, the shifter equivalent of Robocop, basically. Judge, jury, and sometimes executioner. He should be able to handle a little long distance reconnaissance.

"What do you need?" he whispered back.

I told him. He started to laugh, but choked it back and nodded.

I dropped down carefully to make room by the oak trunk for Alek, keeping my profile as low as possible. I closed my eyes and visualized the thicket Harper and Levi were hiding in. I heard the slight shift of clothing as Alek crept up to the tree I'd been hiding behind, felt his warmth as he crouched against my body. I was almost sad Max was lying right there, because suddenly I could think of a lot more interesting things to be doing in the woods on a warm summer day.

Okay, focus. Paintball. Not licking Alek's chin and begging for kisses. Yeah.

I opened my eyes, keeping the image of the thicket in my mind as I looked down at the small pile of paintballs. One of the exercises I do, the only one I kept doing in my twenty-five years of running and hiding from Samir, was to lift multiple stones and form patterns into the air. The paintballs weren't much different than the stones. About the same size, a little lighter.

Usually, however, I had my hands to help me visualize things. I couldn't even grab my talisman, the silver twenty-sided die around my neck, for a focus.

I summoned my power, letting it stream through me in a shivering rush, and lifted one paintball, then another, and another, until all eight remaining were in the air. I sent them up through the trees, as high as I could without losing my thin tether of magic and control. I just hoped I could stretch my magic across the meadow. Too late now to back out of the plan. If this didn't work, I'd have to surrender. No more ammo.

"Ready?" Alek whispered.

I nodded, not trusting speech.

Alek whipped his head out from behind the tree, squinting down the field, his eyes probably picking out details in the shifting shadows of the thicket that I would never know.

A paintball burst on the tree by his head, another whizzed by and splattered on the next tree in.

"Send the balls, I know where they are," he whispered.

I sent my paintballs, still high up in the air, down the left of the field, hoping they would be far out of Harper and Levi's lines of sight. Alek looked around the tree again, this time from the other side.

"Harper is behind that bush with the dark green and white leaves. Levi is crouched behind those two saplings with the twinned trunks."

I peeked around the tree, picking out where he said they were. I saw nothing but slight movement in the leaves of the bush which could have been wind. If Alek was wrong, we'd lose.

Fortunately, in the three months I'd been sharing my bed with him, I'd learned that Alek wasn't wrong very often. And he hated losing almost as much as I did.

In my mind, I gathered the paintballs into two groups of four, pushing on my magic to send one group over the bush where Harper was and the other group around behind the saplings. Their foliage wasn't thick, the trees too young to have many branches. I guess Harper and Levi hadn't thought about cover from above.

Rule number one of horror movies? No one ever looks up.

My magic was holding, though it felt like I had dragged hot wires out of my brain and my power was slippery in my mental grasp. I could see the thin tethers holding the balls in the air, which meant another sorcerer would be able to as well. I filed that information away.

"Geronimo," I said under my breath as I pooled more magic around the balls and shoved them downward as hard as my weakening control would allow.

"Fuck!"

"Holy shitballs!"

The exclamations from the thicket were music to my ears.

Harper and Levi stood up from their spots, their heads and shoulders running with a rainbow of paint colors. In the meadow, Ezee sat up and started laughing.

"You two look like a unicorn took a shit on you," Max yelled, getting to his feet.

"Frag the weak! Hurdle the dead!" I yelled, heaving to my feet and running out into the meadow. I used a bit of power to burn away the baling twine on my wrists and thrust my sore arms out, making airplane noises as I ran in a circle through the grass.

"What are you, an Argentinean soccer player?" Ezee said, still laughing. He brushed at his khaki shorts, though there was nothing to be done about the splatters of paint. Somehow he made them look artsy and cool. Ezee could make any outfit look nice.

"Futbol, not soccer. Geez," I said, grinning.

Paint exploded onto my chest, the balls stinging madly as they burst. I fell backward into the grass.

"Hey," I said as Harper stalked toward me. "I won, no fair."

"Mom has tea ready. Let's go get cleaned up." Harper stuck her tongue out at me and walked toward the large house in the distance.

"Sorry," Levi called out. "Can't trust a fox, eh? Good job with dropping those balls on us, by the way." He offered a hand to his brother and they followed after Harper.

"If only Harper felt the same way," I muttered. "Somebody is a sore loser."

Alek swept me up into his arms and kissed my forehead. "Takes one to know one, eh?"

Laughing, covered in paint, and tired as hell, I pushed him away and followed the others to the house. Another lesson learned, I guess.

I wasn't laughing later when we got back to my place. Alek was still mostly living in his little trailer, which he'd parked out at the B&B at Rosie's invitation, but we spent a lot of nights at my apartment above my game and comics store.

My mail was stuffed in the box by my back door and I saw the postcard even as I picked up the slim pile. Another missive from Samir. Awesome.

"Want me to burn it?" Alek asked as I set the mail on my kitchen table and picked up the postcard.

"No, safer to keep them in the iron box behind wards," I said. Alek was the only one I had told about the postcards, mostly because he'd been there when the first arrived in the mail a mere week after the mess with the warlock.

This one was like the others, only my address and name on it, no message. Just a stylized S. Creepy fucker. The first had been of the Eiffel Tower in Paris. The next showed up a couple weeks later and had a picture of a canal in Venice. The third was another three weeks after that with a bunch of castle ruins from some place in Scotland.

This was the fourth. It was just a photo of a bunch of trees, no small text on the back telling me where it was taken. It looked weirdly familiar, however. I pushed away the shiver that crept over my skin. There were conifer forests like that all over the world. No reason to think it was from around here.

"Sometimes I wish he'd just show up and get this over with," I muttered. I didn't really. Samir would crush me. I was getting stronger, but I had no illusions that I could beat a sorcerer who'd been around since the days when Brutus stabbed a guy named Caesar.

"Every minute he doesn't is good for you," Alek said. "You did well today; you are getting stronger, learning new ways to control your powers."

I smiled up at him. He always somehow knew the right thing to say, even if sometimes I wanted to punch him in the face for saying uncomfortable truths. It was Alek who had postulated that Samir hadn't shown up yet because he was uncertain of me. Alek had a point. I had gone dark for twenty-five years, running and hiding and barely using magic. Samir had almost caught up to me a couple times, but I'd slipped away from him and stayed hidden.

Until three months ago. Then I'd blazed onto the magical map. Alek pointed out that I'd appeared here, near the River of No Return wilderness which had one of the strongest networks of ley lines running beneath its millions of unbroken wild acreage, and living in a town full of shape shifters and other magical beings. From Samir's perspective, this whole thing probably looked like some kind of trap. Why else would I stop hiding if I weren't ready for him, right?

Alek's logic made a certain kind of sense. Samir was arrogant enough to believe his calculated approach to life was the way anyone would approach things. He wasn't the type to risk his life for anyone, so he would never understand or conceive of the choice I'd made three months ago. I could have stayed hidden, but friends would have died, and I would have had to leave the life I'd built here.

I was done running. Hence the whole training to use my powers and pretending that if I did, I could win against Samir.

I knew I couldn't. But I didn't have the heart to tell Alek or Harper or the twins that. They believed in me; the least I could do was try to go down fighting when the time came.

"I'm taking a shower," I said. "Joining me?"

"No," Alek said with regret in his voice. "I'm going to try calling Carlos again." His handsome brow creased in worry. It was Sunday, which meant he usually called and talked to his mentor and friend, a fellow Justice named Carlos. It had been two weeks since Carlos and he had talked, however, and Alek was worried. I hoped he reached him tonight. A Justice going silent was probably not a good sign.

I came out into the living room after showering the last of the paint out of my waist-length black hair and cuddled up to Alek on the couch. I knew from the worry in his blue eyes even before I asked that he hadn't reached Carlos.

"Nothing?"

"No," he said, sliding an arm around my shoulders. "Nothing."

"Wouldn't the Council tell you if there was something to worry about?" I leaned into him, tucking my head against his broad chest, and breathed in his vanilla-musk scent.

"Perhaps," he said softly. He shook his head and took a steadying breath. "I called for pizza while you were in the shower. Half all meat, half pepperoni and pineapple."

It was a sign of how comfortable we were getting with each other that he knew what to get me, especially considering he thought fruit on pizza was an abomination. I wasn't sure how I felt about that, the comfort level or the whole aversion to delicious pineapple.

"You still coming to game on Thursday? You aren't going to dodge it again, right? We're down a man 'cause Steve has that family thing." We'd been trying to get Alek to game with us for months. I'd broken him in to video games, but we'd yet to get dice into his hands.

He sighed. "I'll be there," he said, nuzzling my hair and sliding his hands under my teeshirt.

Which was when someone knocked on the door.

"Pizza!" Alek said, grinning as I pushed my teeshirt back down.

"I'm gonna kill that guy for his timing," I muttered.

Alek opened the door, but it wasn't the pizza man. Instead a tall, wiry man stood there, his eyes sunken and tired looking in his nut-brown face, but his iris's were still the moss green I remembered and his thick black hair was still cropped close to his skull. Just as it had been when I'd last seen him, over thirty years before.

When he told me I was dead to the tribe. When he kicked me out of my home for good.

"Jade," the man said, looking uncertainly past Alek.

"Alek," I said. "Would you kindly slam the door in my father's face?"

Alek didn't end up slamming the door. The pizza guy chose that moment to show up, causing a shuffle of people as we paid him and sent him away, which ended up with all of us standing awkwardly in my kitchen.

"What are you doing here, Jasper?" I asked, emphasizing his name. He didn't get to be called Dad anymore. "How did you even find me?"

My anger wasn't pretty. It burned through me, threatening to boil over, and my magic sang in my veins as I struggled not to do something regrettable. I had thought my resentment, anger, and grief long dead. Guess I was wrong about that. I didn't think Alek would let me blast my father out of existence, however, even if I had truly wanted to. Alek was a Justice and supposed to protect shifters. Dear old dad was a crow shifter. QED and all that jazz.

"I hired a private investigator," Jasper said. He glanced at Alek, who was wisely standing by my side and keeping his mouth shut for the moment. "I didn't expect to find you so close to home."

"This is my home." My father looked smaller and older than I remembered but I knew it was likely time and memory playing tricks on me. I'd been all of fourteen and just a kid the last time I saw him. He was still taller than I, his face mostly unlined in that ageless way older shifters had, where he could be anywhere from thirty-five to fifty depending on expression and lighting.

"Jade," he said, softly this time, his green eyes full of a desperate fire. "I need your help."

I laughed. I couldn't stop it from coming out, the hysterical giggles turning into full blown gasping laughter.

"Go fuck yourself," I said. "And get the fuck out of my house."

"Jade," Alek said, placing a hand on my shoulder. His touch was steadying, even if it pissed me off a little more.

"You stay out of this." I looked up at him as I gained control of my laughter. "That man kicked me out, they all did. Sent me away to live with a woman who was little better than a slave master and her rapist husband. You know the last words that man spoke to me?" I pointed at Jasper. " 'You are dead to the People. You must go away from here and never return.' So don't you go feeling sorry for him."

I hadn't discussed that part of my life with Alek. He knew I'd been on the street, knew about my real family, the four nerds who took me in when I was a teenager and raised me until Samir killed them. I hadn't told Alek about the People. They were a dead part of my life.

"Does Granddaddy Crow know you are here?" I asked Jasper. I figured the old bastard who led the cult that was my former Tribe would know. No one did anything without Sky Heart's say so.

"Sky Heart does not know," Jasper said. "I have come to you on my own. We are desperate."

That surprised me. The Crow who were my former people weren't anything like the Crow tribe, the Apsaalooké, who lived in Montana and were mostly human. Jasper's Crow were all crow shifters, exclusively. Back in the early seventeen hundreds, Sky Heart, a crow shifter and warrior of the actual Crow people, decided crow shifters were special and should live apart. He took a group of them, gathered from many tribes, and went west to finally settle in what became northern Washington State, at a thousand acre forested parcel of land he named Three Feathers. To guard the people and shore up his own power, Sky Heart summoned a powerful spirit, who called itself Shishishiel, the Crow, and from there on out gathered only crow shifters to him. Which involved some fairly underhanded shit like stealing crow shifters from other places, killing those who didn't want to come live with the People, and, oh yeah, kicking out any children who didn't turn into crows.

So, you know, typical cult. I hadn't realized it when I'd been in it, of course. It wasn't until years later when I talked it over with my adopted family that I had seen how dysfunctional they really were. Before that, all I knew was that I was different and had to leave.

"The pizza is getting cold," Alek said. His stomach rumbled.

"So eat it," I said. "Jasper is leaving."

"I cannot leave," Jasper said. "Just please hear me out."

"It cannot hurt to hear him out." Alek turned those big blue eyes of his on me and I sighed.

So we ended up sitting around the kitchen table, Alek eating his pizza, me picking at a slice of mine, and Jasper clutching the glass of water Alek had offered him like it was the last piece of floating wood in a shipwreck.

Part of me wanted to break the ice and ask how Pearl, my mother, was. But I resisted. This man didn't deserve a lifeline like that, nor did either he or my mother deserve my interest or concern.

Finally, after long enough that the awkwardness in the air was as congealed at the cheese on my pizza, Jasper spoke.

"Someone one, or some thing, is killing off the People," he said. "Sky Heart promises he and Shishishiel can stop it, but I think he lies. He says that it is because we have grown too weak, too easy on our young, our blood too diluted with crows who are not Natives. I do not believe this is so."

"You are half white," I pointed out. "Wasn't it Sky Heart who brought in your mother? He is the one who tracks down crow shifters from all over North America and forces them to join you, so he'd be the one to blame if your so-called blood is getting too impure." The whole thing disgusted me. Ruby, my grandmother, had died before I was born, sometime back around World War Two, but my mother had told me about her, about how Sky Heart kept her imprisoned in his home until she bore him a son who changed into a crow. She was where my father got his green eyes.

"Yes," he said, not meeting my gaze. "This is a reason I do not believe. There is magic at work. These murders are not natural. Someone is killing us off and no one will act."

Magic. Samir. No, that would be too easy. If he was killing off my former family to get to me, he'd be gloating more about it. And my father wouldn't be standing here talking to me. He'd be dead.

"Is Pearl alive?" I asked.

"Yes, your mother is fine. But without magic of our own to stop the killing..." he trailed off, eyes still fixed on the water droplets condensing on his glass.

So, not Samir. I took a deep breath. It wouldn't, shouldn't, matter if it were. I wasn't going to help the people who had declared me dead and cast me out.

"What makes you think I have magic that can help you?" I kept staring at him, hard. When I had left, my powers were barely anything. I could occasionally move things with my mind when I was really upset, but that was about it. It wasn't until a couple years later, with the help of my new family and some Dungeons and Dragons manuals to act as focuses, that I'd begun to really work magic.

Jasper raised his head. "Because of what you are," he said. "Because of who your father is."

My chair hit the floor as I jerked to my feet. This was like a bad parody of Star Wars. "My... father? You were my father." I made sure, even in my shock, to keep to the past tense. My chest hurt, as though bands were tightening inside my ribs, making it hard to breathe. Alek rose and picked up my chair, gently pushing on my shoulders until I sat again.

"No. Your mother left us for a while, many years ago." Jasper took a few deep breaths and continued. "After Ruby died, she was unhappy with the People."

"So she escaped," I said. I shrugged Alek's hands off my shoulders. I wished he would leave in the same moment that I was glad he was there. Someone needed to witness the total crazy, I guess.

"Yes," Jasper said the word like it pained him. "She was pregnant when she came back. With you."

Came back? Dragged back by Sky Heart and my father was probably more accurate if I had to guess, but there was no point asking.

"So who is my father?"

"I do not know," Jasper said. He held up a hand to stall my exasperated exclamation. "Your mother says he was a powerful sorcerer. She was sure you inherited his powers. Even as a baby when you were angry we saw things shift and move. Do you not have powers?"

I didn't know if I was relieved by this news. Not being related to the asshole in front of me was sort of nice, but it left me with more questions. And a horrible fear.

"Did Pearl say what this man looked like? Was he Native American at least?" I prayed Jasper would say yes. Universe please, let him say yes.

"Yes," he said and the lump in my throat lessened. "She has said that much. You are full blood, if that worried you." There was bitterness in his tone.

I almost explained. It wasn't that I cared if I had white or whatever blood in me. It was that Samir wasn't Native and for a terrible moment I'd feared that I'd been lovers with my own father. It would have made a horrible kind of sense and be just the sort of twisted fucked up shit Samir would pull.

I didn't owe Jasper any explanations, so I kept quiet about why I asked. Alek's considering stare told me he had guessed my reasoning behind the question. I figured there were some awkward conversations we'd have to have later. Much, much later. After I got Jasper out of my house.

"Shifters are dying?" Alek asked, turning his piercing gaze on Jasper. "Has the Council sent someone?" The Council of Nine was a guardian and governing body for shifters, though no one really knew much about them, not even Alek, who worked for them. The Nine were practically shifter gods, there but not exactly reachable by phone.

"They did, though Sky Heart does not recognize the Nine. A man showed up after the third murder. Our leader had words with him, then the Justice left."

I watched Alek's face as he seemed to do some mental math and that sinking bad feeling started up again in my stomach.

"This Justice, was he a white man?" Alek asked.

"No, black. A huge man, I think a lion shifter from how he smelled. Sky Heart was very angry with him."

Alek moved from the side of the table to loom over Jasper. "When did you see the Justice last?" His tone was intense as he bit off each syllable, his hands clenched into fists at his sides.

"A week ago? No, a little more. It was Friday, I think, so eight or nine days. Why?"

Alek pulled his silver feather talisman that marked him as a Justice out from under his shirt. Jasper's eyes widened but an excited expression came over him.

"Good, you can help as well. We need both of you. Shifters being murdered is Council business, no? No matter what Sky Heart says." His eyes flicked between us.

"The Justice who showed up," Alek said. "His name is Carlos." He looked at me. "I have to go contact the Council."

"What about Jasper?" I said. I knew that this might be Justice business, now that Carlos of the not calling in when he usually did was involved, but no way was this man staying in my home a minute longer than necessary.

"He will come with me," Alek said after a moment. He smiled, his face sympathetic, and I couldn't decide if I wanted to punch him or kiss him. That happens to me a lot with Alek.

"You will consider helping, Jade?" Jasper rose as Alek stepped back, giving him space again.

"No," I said and pretended that the look of despair on his face didn't tug any heart strings. "This is Justice business. They can deal with it."

It was a lie. I knew that if Alek asked me instead of Jasper, I'd go help. Maybe. My wounds weren't healed even after thirty-three years and I wasn't sure I wanted to rip off the bandages. My past was better left in the past.

Alek and Jasper moved toward the door.

"I'll call you or come by tomorrow, yes?" Alek said.

"Okay," I said, leaning up to give him a kiss. I made sure to put tongue in it, hoping it would make Jasper uncomfortable. Guess I'm petty like that.

"Wait," I called after them as they were halfway down the stairs. "How many murders?" I asked Jasper.

"Eleven," he said, his lips pressing into a white line and his expression going flat in a way I remembered from when I was a kid, a flatness that said there was too much emotion beneath for him to handle.

Eleven. When I'd left Three Feathers, there had been about a hundred Crow living there. I closed the door and slid down it to the floor.

Guess it was a good thing I'm a Band-Aid fast kind of girl, because I knew in my heart then, that no matter what Alek found out or what his Council said, I was going back to Three Feathers and the People.

Alek showed up at Pwned Comics and Games, my store, late the next afternoon. I was grateful he didn't have Jasper in tow, but any hope I had of his talk with the Council going well died when I saw the expression on his face. I wasn't sure I'd ever seen him so grim, not even when he'd been pissed at me for trying to run away three months ago instead of facing the evil warlock hurting my friends.

"Bad news?" I asked.

"No," he said. "No news. The Council showed up in a dream last night and told me to stay."

"They showed up? I thought they just spoke through weird visions and feelings and stuff?"

"Usually," he said, running a hand through his white blond hair until pieces of it stuck out at odd angles. "Last night they spoke directly to me."

"So you are staying," I said. It wasn't really a question. Alek was a Justice. He wouldn't go against his gods.

"No. I'm going. Only question is if you are coming with me."

Apparently I can still be surprised by people. I came around the counter and slid my arms around his waist. He smelled good, as always. Solid, warm. He was worth risking things for, worth keeping safe.

"Oh," I said. "Uh, okay." There wasn't much else to say. I had already decided the night before that I would go if the Council wasn't going to take care of things. The People had thrown me out, but they were still people and I couldn't stand by and let them all die at the hands of some crazy murderer. Nor could I let Alek walk into the situation alone.

Especially since I had a niggling feeling that murderer might be Samir, or at least instigated by my psycho ex.

"Good," he murmured into my hair. "I'll be glad for your company."

Yep. Definitely worth risking life, limb, and heart for.

We decided to leave in the morning, early. Three Feathers in Washington State was a ten to twelve hour drive from Wylde, Idaho. Jasper had left ahead of us, as soon as Alek assured him that he, at least, was coming to help.

Alek and I took his truck and his little gypsy-style trailer. I left an annoyed Harper in charge of the store with a promise to call her with updates.

On the ride, Alek filled me in on what Jasper had been able to tell him about the murders. The killer, or killers, was somehow hiding from the expert hunters, and also somehow able to leave the bodies spectacularly displayed where they would be found immediately. Not an easy task in over a thousand acres of old growth forest on the side of the Cascade Mountains.

The method of death? Something a Hannibal Lector fan would approve of, I guess. Removal of the organs was all Jasper would tell Alek. He said we would have to talk to Sky Heart if we wanted to know more.

I had packed light, wishing I had more magical gizmos to bring. Over the last few months I'd been trying to craft some items, but apparently my player hadn't gotten the "craft magic item" feat at char gen. So far my attempts to store magical energy in things had resulted in some impressive pockmarks in my kitchen floor and little else.

I hadn't tapped into the memories that Bernard Barnes, the former evil warlock whose heart and power I'd consumed, had left inside me. It was too gross, too disturbing to see his life laid out in my head and to pick through the madness and murderating for the potential gems of useful knowledge.

For now, I was just trying to work with what I had. Too bad I was a lot better at slinging fireballs than more finessed, useful magic.

I just hoped whoever this killer was, he wasn't immune to fire.

"What am I walking into?" Alek said after I don't know how many hours of diving had gone by. He refused to let me drive his truck, so I stared out the window trying not to think about anything at all until his question pulled me back.

"What do you mean? With the People?" I shifted on the bench seat and stared at his handsome profile.

He nodded, his eyes flicking to me and then back to the road.

"Fuck if I know," I said. "I haven't been there in thirty-three years. I assume a lot of the people are the same, since Sky Heart doesn't let his people go. It's like a cult. Everybody with the same last name, half the people related somehow to the other half except a few people who got dragged in at some point. Mostly Native Americans, few Whites, few Hispanics. Sky Heart is the one who picks people, ordains if they are good enough to be there. And every damn one will be a crow shifter, you can bet on that."

"That's it?"

"What? You want a biography of all hundred or more people at Three Feathers? How old are you, really?"

His eyes flicked to me again. "Sixty-one."

"How much of your childhood do you remember? Can you name what the adults were doing and how they thought about things when you were ten? I was fourteen when I was kicked out. I remember a couple of my cousins, people close in age to me, and I remember my parents. But mostly I've spent all these years *not* remembering."

Alek took a deep breath, then nodded slowly. "All right. I see your point."

"You look good for your age," I said, trying on a smile. I shouldn't have asked his age. It wasn't something us long-lifers did much. Time wasn't the same for us, age wasn't either.

"You, too," he said, his eyes crinkling as he returned my smile. "Veritable spring chicken."

"Craddle-robber," I muttered. The chuckle we shared felt forced, but at least it was something.

We lapsed back into silence and I went back to staring out the window, watching dirt and trees slide by until they blurred, one patch of road the same as another, me trying to not remember as hard as I knew how.

Jasper had given Alek directions, but we didn't need them. Somehow, even thirty three years later, I knew the turn-off, knew the shape of the trees and recognized the gravel road leading into Three Feathers.

Of course, all the "no trespassing" signs with obligatory shotgun holes in them would have tipped off anyone. Sky Heart pretended his land was an official Indian Reservation, though it was no such thing. The locals in the nearest town figured it was, however, and he kept people paid off in the local government to look the other way as well. The humans must have figured it was just a big patch of woods full of crazy Indians and left it at that. The People kept to themselves, homeschooling their kids, living on whatever investments Sky Heart had made and whatever they crafted to sell. Woodworking, pottery, weaving, and game meat had all been popular choices when I was a kid, and I doubt Sky Heart had changed much since.

I guess when you are over three hundred years old and an egomaniacal cult leader, change doesn't really come easy.

I swallowed my bitter thoughts along with the nerves in my stomach as we drove up the main road and approached the group of buildings that formed the core of Three Feathers. The sun was sinking in the sky, its rays limning the treetops and casting long shadows over the huge clearing the road dead ended into.

The big log house was Sky Heart's, though he often shared it with whomever he was sleeping with, and one of its rooms had been the dedicated school room when I was little. Two large pole barns flanked the house, their sheet metal siding stained with rivulets of rust, like old blood. The roofs were new, as were the solar panels decorating them. The People preferred to live as off the grid as they could, so that development didn't surprise me at all.

Dotted further out in the clearing and along paths through the trees were more small cabins and clusters of trailers. Three Feathers could almost be mistaken for a campground. Trucks and a few cars were parked in neat lines beside the pole barns.

Everywhere, there were the People. They came out of the shaded forest and houses, gathering in stiff clusters around the edge of the gravel turn-about where Alek brought his truck to a stop. Most were Native, at least in part. Most were related to each other, and, I guess, to me. Inbreeding wasn't exactly uncommon what with Sky Heart's obsession with the purity of his crow shifters. I recognized many of the faces, though names flitted through my mind like angry birds, refusing to be caught.

The air was thick with tension and I could almost taste the anxiety I read on the faces around me. Lines etched in skin that shouldn't have seen signs of age for centuries, mouth after mouth pressed into pale lines, dark eyes wide and haunted. Knives and small caliber pistols tucked into belts, hands close by, hovering like disturbed insects. Fear reigned here.

Then one face trapped my gaze. Pearl, my mother, was still tall and beautiful, her back ramrod straight and her long black hair pulled tight into two braids, the ends wrapped in red leather. She was near two hundred years old but looked early forties, only tightness around her eyes and small wrinkles at her mouth disturbing her smooth brown skin.

I had a lot of questions for her. I just hoped she had answers that weren't more lies, or that didn't only lead to more questions.

"Time's up," I muttered. "Let's do this."

Alek raised an eyebrow at me. He didn't get the Leroy Jenkins reference, but that was okay. It was mostly for me, to remind myself who I was. Not the girl they'd forced out decades ago, that was for sure.

I opened my door and stepped out as Alek did the same. The sound of a pump-action shotgun being racked drew my immediate attention and I reached inside for my magic even as I turned toward the porch of the big house.

"This is tribal land," the man descending the steps called out, the shotgun in his hands pointed right at Alek. "Go away, or else." He punctuated the "or else" by lifting the shotgun and poking the air with the barrel as though it had a bayonet on it.

Sky Heart was the same as I remembered, though not quite the boogeyman of my nightmares anymore, not after knowing Samir. He was a big slab of a man with red-brown skin, and light blue eyes that were his namesake. His black hair was down to his knees, woven through with crow feathers and brightly colored threads until it looked more like a Plain's Indian headdress than a man's hair. He wore a western style shirt with mother of pearl buttons and jeans with cowboy boots and had the physical and charismatic presence of John Wayne and Charles Manson all rolled into one.

Alek held up one hand and made sure his silver feather necklace was visible. "I am a Justice of the Council of Nine," he said in a tone I remembered from the time we met and he accused me of being a murderer. It's not a tone you want directed at you, that's for damn certain. "I am here to investigate the murders of your people."

"And her?" Sky Heart swung the gun toward me and I think I burned a couple permanent willpower points not blasting him off his feet.

"Hello, Granddad," I said instead. Technically he wasn't my grandfather, something I hadn't known until Jasper did the whole reverse Darth Vader thing on me, but it still felt satisfying to see Sky Heart's face tense and then squeeze into an unattractive expression of disgust.

"You are an exile," he said.

"She's with me," Alek said at the same time. "We have questions for you, if you'd prefer to answer them inside." He motioned at the house after casting a pointed glance around at the growing crowd.

"You, I will talk to," Sky Heart said. "Not her."

"It's fine," I said to Alek. "I'll talk to people out here."

He looked unhappy about it, but nodded, seeing the logic, and followed the already retreating Sky Heart into the house. The people around us started moving again, and a hum of low conversation buzzed in my ears, the words blending together but the sounds giving off impressions of hope and fear mixing like oil and water.

"Go on, all of you," my mother said to the crowd, making a shooing motion with her hands. "You've got better things to do than gawk."

I recognized my two cousins standing near Jasper, John and Connor. The infamous two who had led me into an abandoned mine when I was very small and left me there, lost and alone. I'd gotten Wolf out of the deal, so it wasn't all bad. They looked like men now, not the gangly boys they had been when I had left. They didn't meet my gaze, turning away at Pearl's shooing, and fading back into the trees with most of the rest of the People.

One girl didn't. She hovered at the edge of the nearest pole barn, her face somehow familiar to me even though she couldn't have been older than her early teens. Shifters can live for hundreds of years, but until about twenty or so, they age at the same pace as humans. The girl had chin length black hair and deep green eyes, the only anomaly on her otherwise perfectly Native American face. Her lips were wide, her nose straight, her cheekbones high and sharp.

She looked a bit, well, like me.

"Fuck," I muttered. I looked at Pearl. "Tell me that's not your daughter?"

Pearl stepped forward, her dark eyes inscrutable. "Emerald," she said, waving at the girl, "come meet your sister."

In the last two days I'd learned that my father wasn't my father and now I had a sister. Awesomesauce. And someone was kind of literally decimating these people. Double awesomesauce.

"I'm Jade," I said.

"She's not my sister," said Emerald, who was clearly the latest victim of our family's rock-centric naming scheme.

"Half, I guess," I said, dishing out a glare for Jasper.

"You told her?" Pearl said, her lips pressing into a line.

"She needed to know. Where have the lies gotten us?"

"Yeah, about that," I said.

"Not here." Pearl turned and walked away.

Emerald gave me a searing once over with all the scorn a teenager could muster, and stomped after our mother.

I had little choice but to follow.

They say you can never go home again, but I think that's more for poetic value. That or it should be changed to "you really shouldn't go home again" which applied a lot harder in my case.

Our home was a three-bedroom log cabin and the kitchen and bathroom were about the only thing that had been updated since the seventies. The eighteen seventies. The walls were logs and decorated with woven blankets that had been here when I was a kid. The couch was different; our old one had been dark blue, but this had the same heavy Victorian style that looked opulent and sucked to sit on. I chose a handcrafted kitchen chair instead.

"Who was my father?" I asked. No point in small talk. I didn't care how they were doing. Besides, I could see how that conversation would go. Hi, how are you? Oh, in danger of being horribly killed, and yourself? Yeah. No.

"Is she really my sister?" Emerald said.

"Go to your room, Em," Jasper told her.

"Why? Who is she? She's not Crow."

"No," I said, forming a small ball of purple fire in one palm, "I'm something much, much cooler." It was more prestidigitation than real magic, but flashy. The stress was getting to me and I felt the need to be petty and push back a little. To remind these people I wasn't just a kid anymore.

"Shit," Em said, her green eyes going wide.

"Em, language! Jade, please," Pearl said in a perfect "cut it out" mother voice.

"Let the kid stay. She should learn how fucked up we really are, eh?" I looked at Em and offered her a wry smile. She couldn't have been much older than fourteen or fifteen, but I wasn't sure if she had changed yet, had found her inner shifter animal. Just because her parents were crow shifters didn't mean she would be. I hoped for her sake that she was.

Em flopped down onto the couch and gave her parents a stubborn look. Jasper sighed, and Pearl sank down onto one of the other kitchen chairs. Their movements had the feel of habit, of set pieces shifting on a stage.

"He gave his name as Ash. He was maybe Shoshone or Blackfoot," Pearl said, wiping her hands on her sundress and leaving sweaty streaks behind on the green cotton. "I don't have answers for you, Jade. I'm sorry."

Sorry? Fuck this. I rose from my chair and paced the short distance to the kitchen window. The view was as I remembered, too, from all those evenings doing dishes standing in this very spot. My life seemed layered onto itself, past and present swirling into an unreality. I had never thought to be back here, so I'd never mentally prepared for this moment. I turned back to them.

"You just ran off, slept with some random Indian dude, and then came home?"

"I was confused, lost, and he gave me a lift. It was a strange time for me, after Ruby died." She shrugged. "I didn't know I was pregnant until Sky Heart brought me back. I had no way to contact your father anyway, and I hoped, well…" She trailed off. It was clear what she had hoped. She had hoped I was a crow shifter, not whatever my father had been.

"He was a sorcerer?" I asked. It wasn't like there were a lot of sorcerers in the world. We tended to kill each other off, or get hunted down and killed by other people. Gaining power by eating the hearts of other magic users doesn't exactly make us a popular bunch.

She nodded. "He could do things, like light a fire with just his will. No words, no rituals. He was... special." The wistfulness in her face was there and gone again like a shooting star, but I didn't think I'd imagined it.

For a long moment, no one spoke. Em stared at her sneakers, chewing on her lower lip. Jasper slipped his hand into Pearl's and she pressed imagined creases out of her dress, not meeting my eye.

What was there to say? So Jasper wasn't my dad. Oh well. He hadn't been my dad for over thirty years. This family wasn't mine anymore; they'd given up that claim pretty spectacularly by kicking me out and dumping me with an awful woman and her rapist husband.

Yet, here I was. So, I wanted to say, how 'bout them murders? I repressed a nervous giggle.

"Thank you," Jasper said, looking over at me finally. "For coming. Sky Heart won't admit it, but he has grown old and tired. I am not sure he can keep us safe this time."

Em looked up at him with a gasp. "Dad," she said. I guessed she didn't hear him talk negatively about the supreme leader very often.

"Wait," I said. "What do you mean, 'this time'? Has this happened before?" That would have been, you know, good to know. My frakking family and their frakking secrets. It was getting old.

He and Pearl exchanged a look, then both glanced at Em, then turned their gazes back to me. Again it felt like players on a stage, moving from cue to cue for an audience, only now it seemed the play was hitting the climax, but the actors couldn't remember their lines. Jasper's thin shoulders hunched and he looked a decade older as he opened his mouth to answer, though his eyes told me what his words would say before he spoke.

He didn't get a chance to speak.

Screams tore through the quiet clearing and a woman ran toward the big house, crying out for Sky Heart.

We bolted from the cabin and across the gravel drive. My family's house was close to Sky Heart's, given their direct blood ties as well as status in the tribe. Close enough that I had made it onto the big house's porch by the time Alek and Sky Heart came through the door.

Close enough to hear the woman's first coherent words.

"He's dead. It's happened again. He's dead. Dead."

The body was staged just beyond the furthest out trailer in a recently cleared area at the edge of the older trees. There were a couple of large rocks and a tree stump that had been dug around but not cut from the ground yet and hauled away. It was next to that stump that the man's body was staked out.

I felt an odd tingle on my skin as we crossed into the clearing and filed away the sensation for examining later. The air was eerily still and the sinking sun shot weak red-tinged light through the trees, spearing the corpse.

"Back," snarled Sky Heart as other people tried to follow him closer. Jasper and two other men turned and held out their arms, pushing away the growing crowd.

Alek and I ignored them all and approached the body. He was middle aged, which meant he was one of the older residents. His face seemed familiar, but I couldn't place a name to it. His eyes were open, clouded and reflecting only sky. There was a tiny trickle of blood dried at the corner of his pale lips.

The air was thick with the sweet smell of blood underpinned with feces and dirt. The man's plaid shirt was ripped, his hands staked through with large iron nails but there wasn't much blood on them. His nails were dirty and broken. My brain took in details, eyes looking everywhere but at the mess of his chest. Until his chest moved.

"Fuck," I yelled, jumping back.

Alek, cool as always, didn't even flinch, just gave me a sideways look before bending over the body. I moved back up beside him and forced myself to look, to really see.

His chest had been ripped open, like something from a B-grade horror movie, his ribs grey and brownish with drying blood, broken and protruding into the open air. Pinned inside his chest, where his heart and lungs should have been, was a live crow. Its beak was wired shut and its wings were stuck through with crude iron nails, but the poor thing still struggled, its feathers soaked and sticky with blood.

Alek reached into that nightmare and broke the crow's neck.

"Were they all like this?" he asked Sky Heart.

Sky Heart nodded, fingering a small leather and bead bag that hung around his neck. "Yes," he said. He looked in that moment as Jasper had described. Old. Tired.

"Is this how it happened before? Years ago?" I asked. It was a guess, going off what my parents had been talking about before this new murder interrupted us.

He jerked as though struck and looked at me, hate creeping into his pale eyes.

"Before?" Alek asked, rising to his feet.

"This is Crow business. Shishishiel will protect us. This is not for outsiders to interfere."

"Yeah, 'cause Shishishiel the great crow spirit dude is really doing a bang-up job so far, right?" I glared at him, refusing to be intimidated anymore. Jasper had been right about more than one thing. Something unnatural was at work here.

Killing a shifter isn't as hard as killing a sorcerer. You don't have to eat their heart, for example. Decapitation will do the trick, or just a large amount of physical damage all at once. Like exploding someone's chest and removing their heart and lungs and stuff. That seemed pretty effective. Not an easy thing to do, however, to a man who could turn instantly at will into a bird and fly away. A man who would have hundreds of years of experience, be stronger and faster than a human, and who could tank a lot of damage.

"You will be gone from this place by nightfall," Sky Heart said to Alek, though he pitched his voice loudly enough that I'm pretty sure the whole camp could hear him. "And you will take that woman with you."

"Shifters are dying," Alek said. "I will be going nowhere until that stops. You can either help or get out of my way. I obey the Council, not you." He was standing up to his full six foot six height and had turned on his Alpha power, as I liked to think of it. Waves of it radiated off him like heat on asphalt and for a moment it was as though the huge white tiger that was his alternate shape lived just beneath his skin, his ice blue eyes the eyes of an apex predator, his muscles tensed and ready to make the kill.

Sky Heart seemed to shrink under that power, but he clutched the beaded bag around his neck and pressed his lips into a line. "I must discuss with Shishishiel," he said loudly, and then added so quietly that I barely heard him, "please, give me tonight to think on this."

I couldn't recall a time in my childhood that Sky Heart had ever said please. Score one for Alek, I suppose. Or score one for how dire this situation was. That was a pretty uncomfortable thought. Shishishiel was a powerful spirit, but these murders weren't stopping without additional help, that much was clear.

I turned from the staring contest as Alek nodded and forced myself to look more closely at the body.

"Who was he?" I asked.

"Mark, my husband," the woman who had broken the news said. I hadn't heard her approach but she stood, thick shoulders shaking and eyes runny with tears, not ten feet away.

Most of the People are named pretty generic names. It keeps it easy for records when they have to pretend to be further on generations of who they really are. There are a lot of biblical disciples in there, Matthews, Marks, Lukes, and Johns. For the women, flower names are pretty usual. Except in my family, of course. We all get rocks. The way the People often differentiated one John or Luke or Rose from another was using nicknames.

"Redtail," I said, half question, half vague recollection from decades ago.

"Yes," she sniffled. That made her Mary, or Marigold, I thought. Some things from childhood were so clear, other things faded away and lost. Sadly, the clear things were pretty much all the awful, hurtful parts.

I looked away from the grieving woman and tried to look at Redtail in a clinical way. *CSI: Magic edition*, right? I could do this. I concentrated, bringing up a little power, trying to figure out what I wanted to know, to see. There wasn't a Dungeons and Dragons spell for figuring out how someone was murdered, was there? Nothing came to my mind.

I thought about how I could see my own sorcery, about how Samir used to demonstrate things to me and I could see and feel his power, familiar but different. Like how warm water and cold water are both water, but not the same to the touch.

So. Detect magic. That's what I needed, for the moment. I pushed on my power as I closed my eyes, visualizing it in my head as coating my sight and giving me the ability to see what I should be able to only sense.

In DnD, detect magic can be dangerous. If there is too much magic or the spells used around you are too high of a level, you'll knock yourself out. I hoped that real life wasn't like that. With the warlock who had tried to kill my friends, I'd been able to sense his magic as a wrongness, like smelling rot or mold even if you can't see it.

I opened my eyes and looked at the body. Nothing. Maybe I was failing to do what I wanted to do, magically. There were no other sorcerers around to cast a spell so I could see if it was working. I hadn't been able to sense the warlock's magic until I touched his victim. I really didn't want to do that, but if it would help, if it would save lives, well… Part of being an adult is doing things you don't want to do, right?

I swallowed bile and tried to not breathe as I bent down over the body and laid my hand on his arm. Fuck adulthood. His skin was cold. Very cold. Like he'd been frozen. A deep shiver twisted my spine, locking up my muscles for a moment, and darkness crept in at the corners of my vision. Then the world turned white, trees and sky and ripped up body disappearing under a blanket of freezing white light.

"Jade." Alek's voice and warm hands brought me back. I wasn't touching the body anymore, instead I was feet away, Alek holding me in his arms as I lay half prone on the churned up ground.

"Rage," I muttered. My tongue felt too thick, my mouth full of sourness, and an unnatural cold, deep hatred still rang inside me. "Something is really angry, and it isn't normal." I wasn't sure I was making much sense.

Alek lifted me up. "You're freezing," he muttered. "I'm taking her to my trailer. We will talk later, after you have spoken to your Crow spirit," he said to Sky Heart.

I let Alek carry me like a damsel in distress all the way back to his little home on wheels, my mind slowly unfracturing as I tried to parse what had happened. There was magic at work, which I guess was pretty obvious from the whole exploded chest thing. It wasn't sorcery though, not my brand of it. It wasn't anything I had any experience with, which wasn't saying much, alas. I'd spent the better part of twenty-five years running away from Samir and avoiding magic and magical things at all costs. I didn't exactly have a talking skull or a giant library of musty tomes to research this stuff. Just impressions and guesses.

I pressed my face against Alek's chest, his shifter warmth seeping slowly into my body. I was supposed to be at home with my friends, leveling up in anticipation of all of us getting killed by my psycho ex, not back reliving childhood trauma and playing amateur detective. It wasn't fair. Sky Heart and the People had cast me out. They deserved whatever they got. It wasn't my problem.

Whining about my lot in life and blaming the victims of terrible crimes? Weird.

I called up my magic again, letting it flow through me, this time for warmth and to purge all feeling of whatever it was I'd sensed on Redtail's corpse. I'm not a stranger to self-pity parties, but the anger rising in me felt off, unnatural. My power shoved it back, pushing away the cold and the resentment until I felt more like myself.

Rage. Resentment. Hatred. All lingering strongly on the body of a man who had probably felt none of those things. I doubted it was his ghost or spirit.

I didn't know much about spirits, but I knew some. Samir had been interested in all that stuff. He had multiple giant libraries full of musty tomes, though I'd ever only seen one in person. He had kept me away from the book learning, being uninterested in me gaining real knowledge. He had only wanted me to gain power, the way the witch in fairytales fattens the kids before nomming down on them. There were sort of such a thing as ghosts, but they were more impressions than really the dead still somehow living on. Strong emotions, big events that were usually traumatic, powerful people dying, that kind of thing, all that could create a spirit. How powerful the spirit was and what it could do depended on how powerful the event or person creating it was.

Alek set me down to unlock his door and I managed to stay on my feet. My body felt like I'd been punched repeatedly, but my magic had warmed me and cleared the cobwebs from my head. I was able to mount the handful of steps and enter the little cabin under my own power.

The trailer he lives in is very small, about a hundred and ten square feet. It's efficient, with a kitchenette on one side, a small gas heater and fold-out table and seats on the other, a bathroom at the back, and a ladder, leading to a sleeping loft, built up against the inner wall. Books were piled on cubby-like shelves built into the walls alongside jars of tea and dry goods. The whole place smelled of cedar, beeswax, and bay oil. Cozy, especially given Alek's size, but he moved about the tiny space with the ease of long familiarity.

I sank into one of the padded seats as soon as he'd unfolded it and leaned against the wall. Alek held up a hand and his face grew flat with concentration. A shimmering layer of power slipped up the walls, warding off the trailer. I knew no one would be able to overhear anything we said. Smart. That's why they pay him the big bucks, I guess.

"It's not Samir," I said. "Not a sorcerer; that I'm pretty sure of. But we are dealing with magic."

"You should warn me before you do things," he said with a shake of his shaggy blond head.

"You were busy with your who-is-the-alpha staring contest. I didn't want to interrupt. Besides, why else would I touch a corpse? The whole 'doing magic now' thing was pretty obvious, I'd think."

"I'm going to get you a shirt that says 'does not play well with others'," he muttered.

"I think I own that shirt," I said, trying to smile. "Get Sky Heart one instead. Then we can be twinsies." That got me a wry grin before he turned around and turned on the gas stove.

"So what are we dealing with?" he asked as he filled a kettle for tea.

"Besides a narcissistic cult leader?"

"Jade…"

"A spirit, I think. All I felt was this horrible freezing rage. Not like a hot anger, the kind that flares and burns out. This was real hatred, true rage." I knew, because I'd felt something similar once.

Listening to your family die horribly while you could do nothing to stop it? Yeah. That'll cause a feeling like the one I'd just touched.

"Could a spirit affect the physical world like this without an intermediary?" Alek took the other seat and unfolded the table between us.

I tipped my head back against the wall and shut my eyes, trying to recall everything I could about spirits and the way they worked. I sort of had one following me around, after all, so you'd think I would know more. But Wolf was special, a creature outside of reality in many ways. She would probably know all sorts of things about spirits, but if she could speak, she certainly hadn't demonstrated it in the last forty years. I thought about my guardian more and sighed.

"I don't know," I said. "I don't think so. Wolf can't do much about corporeal threats, only help with magic stuff as far as I can tell. I don't know what rules the Undying follow, if any, but it seems likely that something or someone is enabling this spirit or using its power."

"Not Sky Heart," Alek said with certainty in his tone. "He is terrified but he will not tell me anything. He speaks in half truths. Carlos went away, but I do not think he went far."

The kettle whistled and Alek prepared tea. I closed my eyes again and made myself remember the feelings I'd touched, the look of the scene, how the body had been cold, how it had smelled. Blood. But there hadn't been that much blood on the ground. Killed elsewhere? I thought so. Redtail was a large man, weighed two-twenty easily. Not easy to move. And how did the killer stake the body and put a live crow into the chest so close to the trailers without someone hearing them? In daylight.

I could see why Jasper was convinced there was magic at work here. It was pretty obvious no normal human was doing this. Too many ways a human could fuck it up and wouldn't be strong enough to manage it on their own. Even more than one human would have left a trace, might have caught attention.

"What did you smell?" I asked as Alek set down an earthen mug steaming with jasmine tea on the table and pushed it at me.

"Blood," he said. "Like in a slaughterhouse. Earth. Feces, I think from the body. I sensed no power, saw no obvious drag marks. It is odd."

"And the body was cold. Too cold. How did it get there? We know nothing." I wrapped my hands around my mug, willing the steam and warm ceramic to push away the last of the chill clinging to me. "But the pageantry," I said after a moment. "That feels human to me. It's a statement."

"But what is the killer trying to say?" Alek sipped his tea and a line formed between his blond brows.

"Hi, I'm totally bug-fucking crazy?" I resisted the urge to take my thumbs and smooth the line away.

"But not all powerful, or the killer or killers would strike more often, no?"

"Unsub," I said. "We should call him or her the unsub. That's what they do on TV. Didn't they teach you that at Justice Academy?"

"Unknown subject," he said, the corners of his mouth turning up in a faint smile. "Sure, along with how to use a toothpick and some gum to build a nuke, how to run counter-surveillance maneuvers, make crispy bacon, and kill someone with the five-finger death punch."

I grinned at him. My friends and I were clearly rubbing off on him if he could make jokes like that in a situation like this. My grin died quickly, however, as I remembered something else.

"I don't think Sky Heart can talk to Shishishiel anymore," I said. "When I was little, I remember I could sense the spirit with him, like vast wings unfurling at the edges of my vision. Something has changed, and I don't think it is just that I'm older now."

"I know," Alek said. "He was lying about consulting the Crow spirit."

"What else did he lie about?" I asked. Alek had powers beyond just normal shifter powers, though I didn't know what all of them were. He could do wards, like the one protecting us from eavesdroppers, and he was a walking lie detector. That latter part was a little annoying in a relationship, but it came in handy other times. Like now.

Scratch, scratch, scritch. Our heads whipped toward the door. I summoned my power, preparing a nice bolt of welcome as Alek rose and moved into position. I stood up on the seat, wincing as it creaked under my weight, but keeping my eye and the summoned magic in my hand at the door over Alek's broad shoulders.

One hand drawing his side-arm and holding it at his thigh, Alek swung the door open and turned sideways to make sure we both had clear shots.

It was Emerald, my half-sister. She held a towel that looked to be wrapped around something and looked up at us with huge, scared green eyes.

"Please," she whispered, then she cast a furtive look over her shoulder. "The kids. You have to find them."

After we ushered her inside, Alek offered Em the seat he'd been in but she shook her head, setting the bundle down on the table and unfolding it. Inside were three items. A teddy bear, hand sewn from the look of it. A hairbrush with dark hairs still caught in it. A braided friendship bracelet.

"These belonged to the kids. So you can find them." Em looked at me, her green eyes wary.

"What kids?" I asked, forcing my breathing to normalize and my hands to stop shaking after the adrenaline hit I'd just given myself.

"This is where you live?" She looked around the trailer as though she hadn't heard me.

"Phenomenal cosmic power," I said. "Itty-bitty living space."

Em gave me a blank look and then glanced toward Alek where he leaned on the kitchen counter with an expression that asked if I'd always been nuts or not. I guess the reference was lost on her. Probably one of the few kids in the entire United States who hadn't been raised on Disney movies.

"What kids?" Alek repeated, gifting me with a slight shake of his head.

"The fledglings. Like me. There are three others. They've all gone missing," Em whispered, glancing around again.

"The trailer is warded, no one can hear us," I said.

She hunched her shoulders, the news not relaxing her like I thought it would, and cast another look toward the door.

"Should we go invite Pearl inside?" I asked. I wasn't sure how I felt about her using Emerald to talk to us, but maybe she thought we'd be more sympathetic to a kid. Or maybe she worried that I wouldn't listen to her after what they'd done to me. Or she was a coward. I mentally filled in the bubble for option D: all of the above.

"No," Em said, her hands coming up like a suspect surrendering to the police. "Please. Grandfather is already angry with dad over him leaving and bringing you here. I can't get mom in trouble, too. I'm a fledgling, nobody will be too mad at me for being curious about you."

"The kids are missing?" Alek said, his voice taking on a slight growl now.

Right, the kids. Probably more important than family politics. I swallowed my opinions on my mother and tried to look attentive and open.

"Grandfather says they are dead, that the evil spirit got them because they didn't obey, but mom thinks they are alive. She said with these things that your magic could find them if they are. Can you?" She put that last question out there with a defiant jut of her chin.

Pearl was right, but I wondered how she knew that. She had clearly spent more than just a night or two with my biological father if she knew things that sorcerers were capable of and how our magic might work.

"Yes," I said. "I probably can. You said they are fledglings, so they haven't shifted yet?" She'd said other fledglings, which meant she hadn't, either. It made me a little sad and a lot angry. Her fate in the Tribe was unknown, then.

"No, they are too little. I will be Crow any day now, dad said so."

"I hope he is right," I said softly.

"When did the children go missing?" Alek asked.

"Thomas and Primrose disappeared two weeks ago, after Night Singer got killed. Peter," she said, then stopped and took a quick gulping breath. "He went beyond the boundary stones a couple days ago. Said he could hear Thomas calling to him. They are cousins and almost the same age. That's Peter's hair brush."

"Boundary stones?" I thought of the tingle I'd felt when approaching Redtail's body.

"Grandfather set them, to protect us from the evil."

"Bang-up job he's doing, too," I muttered.

"Grandfather and Shishishiel will protect us," she said. She spoke the words with the strength of a zealot, but the quiver in her chin and the desperation in her eyes turned them from conviction into prayer.

I hurriedly asked another question, not wanting an argument. "Your parents said something about this happening before, do you know when? And what happened?"

Em shook her head and wrapped her arms around herself. "I've heard some of the elders talk about it, but they always shut up when they notice me. It was a long time ago, like a hundred years or something, I think."

A hundred years. Long before my time as well. I sighed and looked at Alek. "Without more answers from Sky Heart, I don't see how we can help."

"You can't find them?" Em asked. Her face closed off again, eyes narrowing, lips pressing together into a pale line.

"I can try," I said. "But we don't know what we are facing out there."

"We will look for them," Alek said. I raised an eyebrow at him and he shrugged as if to say "what else can we do?"

"Okay," Em said, edging toward the door. "Can I go now?"

"Yes," Alek said, cutting me off before my mouth was half open to ask more questions. He pressed himself to the side and let her squeeze by him.

"She was our best source of information," I said.

"She's a kid and she's terrified. We have a direction to go in now. Perhaps if we find these children, Sky Heart will allow us to help."

Fat fucking chance of that. I didn't say so, there was no point. Alek was right. Finding the kids was something I could help with, something tangible to do besides sit around and wait until more people got killed.

If the children were alive. Visions of little bodies gutted and splayed with crows struggling in their bloody chest cavities swarmed my mind. I shoved them away. The evil spirit, as Em had called it, liked to be dramatic. If the children had been murdered, they would have been left where the tribe could find them, wouldn't they? I hoped that wasn't my brain engaging in wishful thinking mode and trying to put order and sense where there was none.

"Fine," I said, looking at the three sad items that represented three lost and probably dead kids. "Let me finish my tea and then we can go look for them."

"No," Alek said, sinking down into the seat across from me. "Not tonight. First light. We should not go wandering around unknown woods in the dark. Alive or not, one night should make little difference, no?"

I hated that he was right, but he was right. I had known these woods well over thirty years ago. But forests are not static, they live and breathe and change. Stumbling around half-familiar land in the middle of the night was a good way to get hurt, even without an evil spirit that could incapacitate a shifter running around.

The woods weren't the only thing around me that was half-familiar and yet irrevocably changed. It took me a long time to fall asleep, even with Alek's familiar warmth and his musky vanilla and clove smell making me feel safer. His calm presence didn't banish my resentment, my old anger. Laying there in the dark, I wasn't sure anything could.

We slipped out of the trailer as soon as the sky lightened. It would get warmer later, but the morning air was crisp and cool, and dew dampened the grass and ferns, glittering like tears in the early morning sunlight. My hair was in a tight braid down my back and I put on a kerchief over my head to protect from branches and brambles. Jeans, a Half-Life tee-shirt, and sturdy hiking boots rounded out my outfit.

I had pulled hairs from the brush and twisted them into a knot so I could tuck them into a rubber band on my wrist and have my hands free in case I needed them. We had decided to use Peter's hair, since it was the most personal thing, being a former part of the boy's body, and because he was the most recently missing, which we hoped meant we'd find him alive. The plan was to cast the spell, follow it to Peter, and if he wasn't with the others, to return and do it again until we found them all.

We didn't really have much of a plan for dealing with the spirit if we found it beyond "kill it with fire" or something similar. I wasn't sure how we'd accomplish that. Not that I was bad with fire, fireball being one of my magical specialties, but using it in the woods seemed like a terrible idea. I looked around for Wolf, but my guardian was nowhere to be seen. She came and went as she pleased, but her absence made me uneasy. She was probably the best defense I had against a spirit. I hoped she'd show up sooner rather than later, but had to trust if I got in real trouble she'd appear. She always had before.

Alek and I had agreed to play it by ear and hope our combined strengths could deal with it. I wished I had time to figure out how to make a knife or something "ghost touch" like in the DnD manuals, but enchanting items hadn't ever been one of my fortes. It was possible, however. Anything was possible with sorcery, provided you could focus the power and summon enough of it.

I pushed away the thoughts of what we couldn't do or deal with, grabbed my D20 talisman with one hand, and focused on the knot of hair strapped to my other wrist. My magic flowed through me and I pushed it into the knot, casting the tracking spell. The spell was pretty crude, telling me only direction. The knot pulled on me, pointing the way, leading us into the woods.

We moved cautiously for a while, passing through the warded boundary of the camp. I spotted one of the boundary stones, now that I knew to look for it, and made a mental note to come back and examine the hunk of white granite when I didn't need my focus to keep the tracking spell going.

The woods were quiet. No insect or bird sounds. Even the brush didn't seem to shift or rustle except where we disturbed them and there was no wind. The spell pulled us north and a little west from the houses, into older woods, the underbrush falling away as the canopy above grew denser. It was easier to move here, but dimmer. The dead lower branches of the coniferous trees stuck out like accusing fingers, jabbing at us and obstructing longer distance vision.

We'd been walking carefully along for at least an hour, not speaking, just following the spell. Alek drew up beside me and held up his hand. I stopped and looked around, keeping my concentration on the knot of hair but trying to peer into the dim forest. I heard nothing for a moment, and then the sound of footsteps, the crunching of dead pine needles and the snap of little sticks.

"Carlos?" Alek called out, his ice blue eyes focusing on something I couldn't yet see. "Wait!"

The footsteps sped up, retreating. Alek took off after them. I started to follow but a flash of red caught my eye. Emerald, in a red sweatshirt, moving parallel through the woods with us. What the fuck was she doing here? I had to get her to go back before she ended up missing or worse.

"Em, damnit! Come here." I turned and waved at her. She shook her head and ran off in a different direction than Alek had gone.

I didn't even think about what I was doing and charged after her. She was only twenty or thirty feet away, I could catch her.

I stumbled through the trees, following the elusive red sweatshirt, muttering curses and calling out to her to come back. A broken-off spear of dead branch swiped my arm, cutting into my skin and drawing blood.

The sudden pain cleared my mind for a moment and I jerked to a stop as the girl in the sweatshirt disappeared. I summoned my power, using it the way I had the night before, pushing it through my body and mind like cleansing fire. It took a lot more energy this time and I felt an intense ball of rage and resentment and confusion push back. It was almost tangible. The spirit.

"Oh fuck toast on a stick," I muttered, looking around. No Alek. No Em, though I suspected she had never been real. The spirit was here and it was royally fucking with us. We'd broken the cardinal rule of adventuring.

Never. Split. The. Party.

I gripped my talisman and kept my power going through me, though I knew between that and holding the tracking spell, I was going to tire sooner rather than later. It was eating more concentration and power than I liked to just hold off whatever that thing was. Better exhausted than dead, I guess. I had to find Alek before the spirit did. No, I wasn't going to think about Alek splayed and dead and bloody and oh fuck.

For a moment I panicked, my heart pounding and blood rushing to my head. I forced the panic down with careful, steady breaths. I could track Alek if I went back to camp and got something of his. I turned and started retracing my steps, eyeing what little I could see of the sky to get my bearings.

The spirit was smart, separating us. Using illusions and deception. I should have expected it from what Em said but with so little information, it was hard to know what it was capable of.

I was learning, though. Boy was I learning.

"Why can't my life be more like a porno than a horror movie," I muttered as I walked. I forced a chuckle at that. If this was a porn movie, with my luck Maid Marion and her Merry Men would show up. I could almost hear Harper quipping, "time for the mandatory girl on girl scene."

I smiled and shook my head. What was I even thinking about? I almost walked into a huge tree as a giant black beast appeared beside me and slammed into my hip, knocking me on my ass. It was a huge beast, the size of a pony, with the head of a wolf, the body of a tiger, tufted ears like a lynx, and, I swear to the Universe, an amused expression in its fathomless, starry night black eyes.

Wolf. My guardian and one of the fabled Undying. Fucking finally. I glared at her, but her furry black face and unfathomable eyes just kept laughing at me. My head cleared again and I swore some more, mostly to make myself feel better as I got to my feet and brushed pine needles off my ass.

I'd lost my grip on my magic and I snatched it back, dragging on the well of power inside. It was so easy to become distracted. More spirit shenanigans. This was getting really frustrating.

"Where have you been?" I said to Wolf. Spirits are something she's supposed to be able to help with, being all magical and shit.

She whined and pawed at the tree I'd almost run into. It looked familiar. It was really two trees that had grown too close together, their trunks twisting and combining as they strained for the sunlight. The kissing tree, we used to call it.

Which meant the old mine entrance was close by. I shivered. Though I'd only been four when my cousins John and Connor got me lost down there on purpose, I still vividly remembered the dank air, the dirty walls pressing in, and the feeling of being buried alive, trapped in a labyrinth and all alone in the dark. If it hadn't been for Wolf, I might never have come out of there.

The mine. It would make a good hide-out if one were a terrible person who didn't mind darkness. It had been boarded up after I'd been lost in it, but still, it might be worth checking. I pushed power back into the tracking spell, recasting it on a hunch. The knot of hair pulled me back to the north, toward the mine. The pull was strong. Peter wasn't far.

Turn back and try to find Alek? Or find the kid? I didn't want to go back into the mine and the spirit was fucking with me pretty hard, despite my magic. I had Wolf with me now, however. And I knew what Alek would want. He'd say to go after the kid. No question.

"This is a terrible idea," I muttered.

Then, one hand on Wolf's thick fur and one pointing out in front of me to guide the way, we went north.

The entrance to the mine was no longer boarded up. The entrance had been cleared recently; brush cut back and the old boards were piled off to one side. The opening yawned in the sunlight like a beast, damp air slightly cooler than the air in the clearing around it seeping out and making me shiver.

At least, I told myself the goosebumps on my arms were from the air.

I called on more magic, focusing it on my outstretched hand and bringing up a brightly glowing ball of golden light. I sent the light ball floating into the entrance. The floor in the opening was scuffed and furrowed, the dirt having long since clogged the tracks that used to run down there. I saw fresh footprints and went to examine them.

A man had come this way. Alek? No, the feet were too small for that. Alek had giant Viking boat feet. It was too much to hope he'd come this way.

The spirit wouldn't have left prints. Wolf didn't, anyway. Perhaps the intermediary we'd speculated about? Gah. I hated that all the things I found just led to more questions. The tracking spell pulled downward. So Peter was in there. Or Peter's corpse.

I looked down at Wolf and took a deep breath. My magic flowed through me and my mind felt clear, so I hoped I was making this probably incredibly stupid decision of my own free will.

"Wolf," I said. "I need you to find Alek. You have to protect him from the spirit or whatever is doing this, okay?"

She whined a little and turned her head east, her nose lifting as she scented the air. She looked back at me as though wondering if I was serious.

"I'm serious," I said. "Please go protect Alek."

With another whine, she vanished. I pulled my light ball back and made my talisman glow instead. Keeping that going while I kept the tracking spell up and kept my head clear of spirit interference was going to suck, but I didn't have a choice. I told myself to just think of this as more practice. If I couldn't handle running a few concurrent spells and finding a lost kid, I had no hope against Samir.

With that cheery thought, I faced the gaping mine entrance.

"I ain't afraid of no ghost," I muttered. It almost made me smile. Almost. Cautiously, I stepped inside, following the pull of Peter's knotted hair down the main tunnel.

The walls changed from earth to stone as I descended. The mine had been active back a century or more ago, but while the shaft dropped at a sharp angle, it was clear of most debris. I would have thought it would fall in after all this time, but the thick timbers reinforcing it held. The ground layer had built up, especially once the opening leveled off a few hundred feet and the first split came.

The tracking spell tugged left, so I took the left channel. Water dripped somewhere ahead. Or maybe behind. It was impossible for me to tell. The glow from my talisman only illuminated a few feet around me. Had Peter just wandered in here and gotten lost? I doubted it. The kids I grew up with used to dare each other about how far we could go in. I'd gone with John and Connor, trusting them and their flashlights, feeling like a really important person that they would let me go along when they normally shut me out of all activities.

The mine had felt like a horrible maze then. It seemed smaller, less ominous now in some ways and even more terrifying in others. Smaller, because I had magic now, a way to defend myself, to get myself out of here. More terrifying because there was a spirit possibly down here waiting to fuck with me. I kept my magic flowing, ignoring the headache that was starting to tighten a vise around my skull. I couldn't afford to get distracted or lost down here, not if I wanted to find the kid and get out again.

Besides, I kinda wanted to encounter the intermediary and kick the unsub's ass. That way I would know they weren't doing something awful to Alek.

I don't know how far underground I went. The tunnel dropped again, branched twice more, and dropped deeper. The walls were all rock now, timbers in the ceiling obscured by darkness, though the height wasn't much and I had to duck. No roots nudged through down here, I was too deep for that, I guess, somewhere into the rocky soil or perhaps even the bedrock.

Then the tunnel opened up, the walls no longer close beside me. The smell of crushed pine needles and cooked meat flooded my nose. The hell?

I pushed more power into my talisman, making more light. The shaft had ended in a cavern, the ceiling somewhere overhead and out of range of my limited sight. I could make out furniture to my left, a table of some kind in the dim edge of my vision. I moved toward it, my glowing D20 casting crazy shadows in the space.

One of the shadows moved oddly in the corner of my eye and I spun to the right, gathering power into a shield. I was too tired, too slow.

I made out the shape of a man before the baseball bat he was wielding smashed into my head. I felt pain, tasted blood, but I didn't see stars. Only darkness.

I came to with the mother of all headaches. I hate getting knocked out and this was the second time in as many days. It's disorienting as fuck. Most knock-outs are pretty quick, not like in the movies where the person goes down and stays down for a convenient amount of time. I had a feeling more time had passed, however. I remembered the hit first, that explosion of pain, then the where and what next.

It was pitch black when I opened my eyes and I couldn't make out a thing. I hoped that meant I was still underground rather than blind.

I took stock of my body, flexing fingers and toes. I was still dressed, but there were restraints of some kind on my wrists and ankles. My arms were pulled back behind and half under me as I lay on my side and my fingers felt swollen, though they wiggled so they weren't totally asleep. With the painful tingling in them, I found myself wishing they were. I tried to push my legs apart, but they were stuck together with whatever was binding me. Something clanked and I guessed I was chained up. The bindings felt rigid enough to be metal. Shit.

I listened, hearing breathing near me. All I could smell was dirt and the faint scent of cooked meat. I figured I had to be in the cavern still, or near it. Pushing through the pounding pain in my head, I tried to call up my magic and bring light into my talisman.

The magic flowed into me grudgingly and hanging on to it hurt so much I whimpered. Something moved near me and I froze as the breathing noise grew closer, almost drowned out by the clack of metal on stone. My talisman didn't light up. I realized I couldn't feel the chain around my neck, couldn't sense the residual power that I stored in it. My D20 necklace was missing.

"Hey," said a soft male voice. "You awake?"

Was it a trap? Probably a trap. I decided I didn't care.

"Yeah," I whispered. "Are we alone?"

"The kids are sleeping, I believe. And I haven't heard the man in a little while," the voice said. He had an accent, very slight, but almost Hispanic in how he accented some syllables and not others. He was near me now, I felt the warmth coming off him, felt his breath as he talked. A hand touched my arm and I tried not to flinch. "You were very beat up, I did not think you would wake. You are not a shifter."

"Carlos?" I guessed, going with the most obvious explanation.

"Yes," he said, a little louder now, excited. "Who are you?"

"Jade, a friend of Aleksei Kirov's," I said, knowing that he and Alek talked all the time. He might know who I was, if Alek mentioned me. I hadn't ever been brave enough to ask. "Alek is here somewhere, in the woods. He didn't come into the mine. Are we still in the mine?"

"Yes, I think so. There's a huge cavern off this area. I heard Not Afraid pacing in there, talking to himself earlier. He is gone now."

"Not Afraid? He told you his name? Is he a shifter?" I tried to remember if I had ever heard of a Crow by that nickname. It rang no bells.

"He and I have talked, a little. When he brings food, and the bucket. He is not a shifter. I don't know what he is. He smells of dead things, old bones, old blood."

I remembered that Alek had told me Carlos was a lion shifter. His hands seemed free; he had touched me after all. "Can you untie me? Can you shift?"

"No," he said and I could hear the head shake that came with it. "We've all got manacles on, hooked into the stone floor. I have a collar on that is also chained down. If I shift, it'll kill me since I can't shift out of it."

"Okay," I said. "Close your eyes. I'm going to make a light."

"Make a light?"

I focused, trying to ignore the headache and my own fear, shoving it all away and focusing on my magic. No hands. No talisman. Well, I'd been practicing for this, right? I summoned a ball of light, just as I had out in front of the mine, though I kept this one small and blue tinted. By choice, not because I was exhausted and out of my element with no hands and no tools. That's what I told myself.

I squinted against the light and looked around me. Carlos knelt next to me, a large black man, heavyset, though it looked to be mostly muscle, with dreads that fell below his shoulders, and golden brown eyes squinting back at me. His hair was a mess of pine needles and dirt and his clothes were streaked with dirt and dried blood. I guessed he hadn't come very quietly. A metal collar with nasty spikes pointing inward decorated his throat and a thick manacle was bound to his leg, both tying him into a heavy ring in the middle of the small chamber with large chains.

Twisting my head to see beyond Carlos, I made out three small shapes huddled against the far wall, a camo-patterned blanket covering all three. A large chain connected to the ring disappeared under the blanket and I guessed they all must be tied to it somehow. One set of eyes blinked against the light, a boy, I thought, though it was hard to tell in the near darkness.

"Peter, Thomas, and Primrose?" I asked quietly as I twisted more, trying to sit upright.

"Yes," Carlos said. He moved as best he could with the thick chain restraining him and helped to prop me up against the cold, damp wall.

"Why are we alive?" I said even more quietly. He was a shifter, I barely had to speak aloud for him to hear me, and I didn't want the kids to overhear us if I could help it.

"This I don't know. I think because we are not crow shifters. He told me I am not a part of things and I would be able to go once he was done." Carlos shook his head. "The kids, I think he is waiting to see if they will change into crow or not."

"That could be a few years," I said. They were pretty young from what I could tell, years younger than Emerald. The knowledge that he had gone out of his way to keep Carlos and the children alive was somewhat comforting. Alek wasn't a crow shifter, so even if the spirit and this Not Afraid guy got him, it didn't seem like his fate would be full of organ removal.

"Time and logic are not things Not Afraid cares for," Carlos said. He smiled briefly, his teeth flashing blue-white in the light.

"Bully for him," I muttered. "I think he's possessed by or working with a spirit. We have to get out of here."

"Would love to, but…" Carlos motioned at his collar and then jiggled his leg, making the chains rattle. "The little ones are only tied by an ankle each as well, and to the same chain. But the steel is new, I can't break it."

He was implying, of course, that if a lion shifter, and a Justice at that, couldn't break the metal, I had no hope. He was wrong. Probably.

Okay, I told myself. All you have to do is destroy the metal. You like destroying things.

The upside of sorcery is it is just raw power. It can be shaped to do or become just about anything if the will is there and if the raw power is there. The downside is that whole having to shape the power and have enough of it in the first place.

There was no way with my hands tied and no focus like my D20 that I would be able to keep up the light and somehow destroy my bindings. With the monumental headache I was nursing, the fact that my body had probably had to reconstruct part of my skull to heal me, and all the magic I'd already expended, I wasn't sure I could even do what I wanted to do.

But I was dead sure that I wasn't going to stay here and shit in a bucket while this Not Afraid dude and his evil spirit cohort slaughtered more people.

I let the light die. "Might want to back up," I whispered to Carlos and waited until I heard him scoot away.

The easiest way to work magic you've never worked before is to have a path for it, a way for your brain to understand and enact the thing you want that won't fuck with your worldview and physics and stuff too much. It was that whole stones and hands problem again. Fortunately, the way I'd learned to control and channel my magic was through Dungeons and Dragons, and DnD has a ton of spells in it. They wouldn't do shit for a normal human, but in the hands of someone with actual magic, they aided my will and imagination, gave me a focus.

Rust Ray is one I'd used as Dungeon Master, not for realsies, on a party and nearly been lynched by the players. They kind of hate it when you destroy their gear.

"Touch attack," I said softly to myself, focusing my power on the manacles around my wrists. I was touching them, so this could work. I pushed my magic at the metal, visualizing it corroding, weakening, rusting away under the onslaught of power. I twisted my arms, putting as much pressure on the metal as I could.

My magic stopped pouring through me, weakening to a trickle as I gasped, straining to hold the spell. My head throbbed and red danced across my eyelids as I squeezed my eyes shut in concentration.

The manacles broke with a discordant clang. I let my magic go and pulled my arms in front of myself, rubbing them to restore full feeling. A million tiny needles pricked at my skin and I turned my lower lip into hamburger as I resisted indulging in more whimpering.

"You all right?" Carlos said.

"Yeah. Hands are free. Just got to get my feet. Hang on." I wasn't sure I could call up more magic, but I did it anyway. If I hadn't spent the last three months training and pulling on my reserves over and over, I don't think I could have managed. Score one for exhaustive practice. Emphasis on exhaustive.

It was easier to rust the manacle on my leg. My hands discovered it was only one leg that was actually chained. The other was tightly duct taped to the metal, and I was able to rip the tape off without resorting to magic.

I crawled to Carlos, feeling for him in the darkness. "Hold very still," I said.

I was ready to drink a horse trough worth of coffee and swear off ever doing magic again by the time I'd broken his collar, rusted out his leg binding, and freed all three children. I wasn't sure I could even walk, my head spun so badly. I managed a small ball of light in one hand and hoped that Not Afraid and his spirit buddy were far, far away. I was in no condition to do more than pass out on them.

Carlos had a rapport with the kids, keeping them quiet as he bundled Primrose, the youngest who looked about six years old, into the blanket and motioned for the others to follow me.

We moved into the large chamber, Carlos sniffing the air and listening before he motioned me to keep going. I wanted to search the cavern for my necklace, but commonsense won out. Escape was more important. I led us back the way I'd come; every step seeming like it went nowhere, the walls tight and cold. One foot in front of another was the best I could manage, my head down, my whole being concentrating on walking and not losing the light.

Then there was light that wasn't mine, daylight dimly piercing the way ahead. The ground had turned upward at some point and I'd been too exhausted to notice. The steep main shaft loomed ahead of me as I turned a corner toward the faint light. Fresh air. Sunlight. Being deep underground will make you appreciate the small things. I had no idea why an adventuring party would ever, ever, ever go into a dungeon. Idiots, clearly.

Just a few more feet, I told myself. Then I collapsed. Warm fur caught me and I heard someone behind me curse in Spanish. Wolf. She was here, under my half-prone body, lifting me up. I clung to her and managed to stumble upward, my thighs burning and my vision blurred to uselessness.

Then daylight. Full, glorious sunlight and the heat of a summer afternoon. We were out of the mine. Now we just had to get the kids back to the camp.

Alek was there, coming toward me with concern in his ice blue eyes.

"I'm okay," I said, hopefully sounding more convincing than I looked. I didn't want to think about how much dried blood was matted in my hair or how dirty I was. My kerchief hadn't survived the head wound. Without needing to hang onto my magic, I felt slightly better. I still leaned heavily on Wolf, but my breathing was coming back under control and my eyes no longer felt like they were squeezing out of my head.

"Alek!"

"Carlos!"

The two men looked as though they might embrace, except Carlos still had a wide-eyed little girl in his arms.

Then Alek looked at me and I guessed from the look on his face that the sight wasn't pretty.

"Are you all right?" he asked, gently touching the side of my face. Blood flaked off and I reached up, wondering where my kerchief had gone.

"You should see the other guy," I said.

"I hope I do," he said, his voice lowering into a growl. His eyes were glacial and promised violence upon whoever had hurt me.

I wanted to throw my arms around him and tell him I loved him right there. My romantic timing sucked, but being hit in the head and chained up underground had apparently clarified some things for me.

"Alek," I started to say but he shook his head slightly, softening the negation with one of his slight smiles.

"Back to camp," Alek said. "Then we will talk."

"I don't know if the kids can walk that far, after being chained so long," Carlos said.

"I can walk," one of the boys said. Peter, I thought. He looked the least pale and weak of the two boys. Two weeks underground and chained wouldn't have been good for anyone, much less a little kid.

"I bet you can," Alek said. "But would you rather ride a tiger?"

Peter and Thomas looked at him, then at each other, then back at him, their dark brown eyes suspicious. "I don't see no tiger," Peter said.

Alek smiled and shifted. One moment he was a huge Viking of a man, the next a giant tiger. Dire tiger, Harper called him. It wasn't a bad description. Shifter animal forms are more like the Platonic ideal of the animal than any realistic version. They are bigger, prettier, stronger, faster. A giant white tiger is one of the most beautiful and most terrifying things ever. Alek was lovely and scary as fuck, is what I'm saying.

Carlos lifted the wide-eyes boys onto his back. A tiger isn't made for riding, but I knew they would cling and Alek would take it carefully. It wasn't like their combined weight would give him back problems.

"I wanna ride tiger," Primrose said, clutching at the blanket.

"How about you ride a lion instead?" Carlos asked her. "You had better ride with her, Jade, keep her on."

It was a testament to how tenuous and dangerous the situation was that he would allow a virtual stranger onto his back. I was about to say I had my own ride, but glanced around and realized Wolf was missing again. Great.

"Come on, Primrose," I said with what I hoped was a nice smile. "Let's ride a lion."

If Alek was a dire tiger, Carlos was definitely a dire lion. His ruddy mane reminded me of Narnia movies and I struggled not to make an Aslan joke. It didn't hurt that my brain was so fried and in pain that I couldn't come up with a good one anyway.

I put Primrose up onto lion Carlos's back and then climbed on. He rose up and I gripped his mane with one hand and held onto the little girl with my other arm. Alek and Carlos moved through the woods in big, ground-eating strides.

It seemed to take no time at all to get back to camp. I felt the hum of the wards on the boundary stones and then we were through the ferns and out of the woods. The People were gathered around the big house, much as they had been when Alek and I arrived.

Sky Heart was there, standing over an indigo-wrapped body laid out on a stretcher. Wildflowers in little bunches were strewn around and the air was solemn, no one talking until we emerged into the big clearing. A woman cried out and ran toward me, reaching for Primrose, who squirmed and called out "Mommy." I let her go, sliding to the ground as Carlos dropped low to let us off his back.

Staggering to keep my feet, I looked up and my eyes met Sky Heart's own. They were red, puffy, and full of fear.

For a long moment we were swamped with people asking
questions, relatives claiming the children. Carlos and Alek
shifted back to human form, but none of us were able to
answer much in the clamor and press of bodies. I swayed
on my feet but forced myself to push gently through,
heading toward Sky Heart. That man had things to
answer for and I wasn't going to be shoved aside like
yesterday. Whatever was going on, I had a strong feeling
it began with the leader of the Crow.

I got through the crowd and stopped, facing Sky
Heart over the corpse.

"Who is Not Afraid?" I asked him. I knew his keen
shifter hearing would be able to catch my words.

"I do not answer to you, exile," he said, the fear in his face morphing into rage as he looked at me.

"Good thing I now have two Justices with me then, isn't it?" I shot back. "You may pretend you are outside all laws, but I hear the Nine don't take well to shifters killing shifters. If you caused this somehow..."

He cut me off with an angry cry like the hunting shriek of a hawk and shifted. His huge crow form lumbered into the air with angry wing-beats, scattering the bunches of flowers and blowing dust into my face. Sky Heart fled into the tall trees surrounding the big house and disappeared among the shadowed high branches.

I stood over the corpse, too tired and shocked to react. A hand touched my arm and I jerked sideways.

"Come," Pearl said. Her dark eyes held only sorrow. "You may use our bath. Then we will talk."

"Damn right we will," I muttered.

She ignored my ungracious comment and led me through the crowd. I caught Alek's eye and he gave one of his gallic shrugs that I took to mean I should just learn what I could and we'd talk later. I hoped that now they had brought the children home safely, the People would be more inclined to let the Justices help, more inclined to share what they knew. Maybe I'm still naïve, or maybe I'd been hit harder in the head than I thought.

I'd been hit pretty damn hard. The mirror in the single bathroom in my old home revealed a thick pink scar along the side of my face that was slowly fading out as my body did its quick healing thing. Bruising would take longer to heal, unfortunately, but at least my vision wasn't impeded by swelling. The side of my head was caked with flaking dried blood, my hair was a nest of pine needles and dirt, and my clothes looked like someone had dragged me over a mud-covered cheese grater. I felt naked without my talisman and rubbed my chest where it usually rested.

Not Afraid had better start being afraid, I thought. I wasn't going to forgive that theft, not that I would forgive the murders either. Or the being hit in the face with a two-by-four or bat or whatever the hell that had been. His list of transgressions was substantial.

I stripped and washed off the worst of the grime before running the hottest bath I could stand and sinking into it. My hair floated out around me like ink and I sighed. It would be a bitch to untangle and braid again, but relaxing completely in the hot water and letting the dirt and blood soak out of my skin was worth it.

Pearl knocked and then came in before I could respond. For a moment I wanted to order her out, but she was my mother still in some ways. She'd wiped my ass as a kid and breastfed me. I didn't have anything she hadn't seen before. Bonus was that it meant I could question her without having to move.

"Why do you stay here? Any of you?" I said. It wasn't the question I'd meant to lead with, but Sky Heart's fear and anger bordered on insane. It was worse than I remembered from when I was a kid. Maybe I just hadn't noticed back then.

"It is our home," Pearl said. "Without Shishishiel to protect us, who knows what might happen. The world is not a very nice place."

I almost started to argue that there was a lot of good out there, freedom, people who didn't throw people out who weren't like them, but then I thought about how it might be for someone who had lived in a bubble for centuries. And I thought, fleetingly, about Samir. There was a lot of evil in the world.

Yet, hiding from it hadn't helped me, and it didn't seem to have helped the People. Evil had still found them.

"Are you sure Shishishiel still protects you?" I said.

"Yes." Her tone allowed no further questions along those lines and I decided to take a hint and drop it. She set down the folded stack of clothing and pulled over a small wooden stool from the vanity.

"Who is Not Afraid?" I asked.

"Where did you hear that name?"

"Carlos, the other Justice. He talked to the guy who has been killing your people. That was the name he gave." I watched her face carefully, but her expression was guarded; only a slight tension about the mouth and eyes giving away any emotion at all, and I wasn't sure what that emotion was yet.

"A little more than a hundred years ago, there was a murder like these ones. It only happened once then, because Sky Heart caught the man responsible and he was executed. That man was called William Not Afraid. He is dead. Whoever this man is, he cannot be Not Afraid." She shook her head emphatically, as though it would help make her words true.

"Who did Not Afraid kill back then?" That was what I envisioned a cop on *Law and Order* asking. Trace the original crime, see what started that, then you could find out why there was a copycat. Of course, cops didn't have to contend with near immortal beings, magic, or spirits. Lucky them.

"Opal," Pearl said softly. "Sky Heart's second wife."

Figured he would be at the center of this. "Did he ever tell you why?" I didn't clarify if I meant Sky Heart or Not Afraid, because I didn't care how she took it. Either would do if she had an answer, so I left it deliberately ambiguous.

"No. It may have had something to do with Not Afraid's twin sister. That is what I have always suspected, but Sky Heart won't speak of it." She looked down at her hands and picked at imaginary lint on her jeans.

"What happened to his twin?" I asked after a moment, when it seemed she wasn't going to continue on her own.

"She wasn't Crow. She was exiled." Pearl kept her eyes down, not meeting mine.

"Not Afraid was Crow?" I asked, thinking of Carlos telling me that he was sure the man who had captured them was not a shifter.

"Yes, but Buttercup was not Crow. She wasn't even shifter, but one of the rare normal human births. She was exiled, sent away to live with missionaries as we usually did then with those who were not People. But Sky Heart wouldn't tell Not Afraid where he had sent his twin, and he wouldn't let Not Afraid leave to find her. They were very angry with each other. Not Afraid seemed insane with rage. They fought and it shook the forest. Sky Heart and Shishishiel had no choice but to kill him."

She looked up then, but her eyes stared past me, right into her memories. I realized I had no idea how old my mother was. Older than I'd thought. I wondered what I would remember in a century or three, what events would stick and what would fade into fog and be lost to me forever.

Buck up, kid, I told myself. *I doubt Samir will let you live that long.*

I closed my eyes and sank lower in the tub. At least I had some information. Carlos had said it was a man and not a shifter. Maybe it was a descendant of the twin. If she had harbored a grudge for her whole life and had children, it was possible she could have passed that grudge on to them and one grandchild or great grandchild had come to collect.

Which didn't explain the spirit, except that the grandchild or whatever was clearly possessed by it. Or working with it. Either way was scary enough, given what the spirit had been able to accomplish through the intermediary.

I must have drifted off. The bath water grew tepid and when I opened my eyes, my mother was gone. I had wanted to ask her more about my birth father, but the moment seemed to have slipped away.

I managed to pull on clothes, wrap a towel around my head, and get as far as the uncomfortable couch. This time it was Em who appeared, holding out a knit blanket.

"Mom said you would want to sleep, if the bath didn't drown you."

"I'm sure those were her exact words," I said and was rewarded with a sheepish smile.

I sprawled onto the couch and crashed hard.

It was dark when I awoke to the smell of coffee and pancakes. Though it was after midnight, Jasper and Pearl invited me to stay and eat something since they had leftovers, but I wanted to go check on Carlos and Alek. Okay, I'll admit, I wanted to get out of that house before any more memories stormed in and gave me unwanted feels. After the day I'd had, I wasn't up to sitting down and having family dinner.

"I don't suppose there is cell phone reception out here?" I asked them before I stepped out the door. I hadn't emailed or texted Harper like I said I would and I knew she'd be annoyed and worried by now.

"No," Jasper said. "Sorry. No cell, no internet. We live our own lives up here."

I managed to swallow about fifty snide comments I could think of in response to that and stepped out the door.

It was a warm night with a light breeze. The big house was all dark and I figured Sky Heart was probably still sulking in the trees. Or standing in a dark room watching his little cult empire crumble from behind tinted glass.

The couch may have felt like it was covered in hide and stuffed with rocks, but sleep had done wonders for my body. I pulled up a thread of magic, just to test how it would feel. No headache, that was good. No talisman. That was bad. It was harder to focus without it and I knew I'd be limited in the kinds of spells I could do without my D20. Maybe it was a crutch, but I missed it. Still, the power was there when I reached for it, so maybe I didn't need the crutch.

Which didn't mean I wasn't going to go get it back as soon as it was daylight.

A faint glow out in the trees to the west caught my eye as I walked across the gravel circle toward Alek's trailer. It was pale and flickering blue, not a light like would come from one of the cabins or trailers in the camp. I remembered the boundary stone from the morning and thought that might be about where it was placed.

Mentally berating myself as the stupid horror movie victim who goes off unarmed into the words to investigate the weird thing instead of ignoring it and heading toward people and safety, I changed course and walked toward the flickering light. Horror movie victims aren't generally nearly immortal with the ability to cast *Fireball*. So, you know, I had that going for me.

The boundary stone wasn't the thing glowing. The light flickered just beyond it, hovering like a will-o-the-wisp among the dark sword ferns and spiky broken branches. I stopped at the stone and peered into the dark.

"Not Afraid?" I called out softly. "Talk to me." Worth a shot and somewhat better than calling out the old cliché "who's there!" right before I get eaten by something big and ugly.

"She is not Crow, but she is here," a young male voice responded, the words faint. I realized he was speaking in the Siouan language that the Apsaalooké, the Native American Crow tribe, used. It was the language some of the elders at Three Feathers had spoken when I was little and didn't want me to understand what they were saying. Their efforts had been useless, since even as a small child I had understood languages I shouldn't have known. It was yet another thing that had set me apart.

"I am not a crow person," I called out in the Crow tongue. "Talk to me, tell me what you want, why you are doing this. Is it for Buttercup?" I added the last part as a guess, hoping to get a reaction.

Not Afraid seemed to materialize from the darkness, only feet away from me. He was very young, not much older than Emerald, and I wondered why Carlos hadn't mentioned that. Perhaps he hadn't seen him clearly. Not Afraid's face was gaunt, his hair ragged and shorn close to the scalp. He wore leather clothing that had seen better days and looked like something out of a Cowboys versus Indians movie. His eyes glowed faintly in the dark with a blue-white sheen over their dark irises and it sent a shiver down my spine. The spirit was definitely a part of him, either by possession or by him working some spell to control it.

I wondered if he even knew who was controlling whom anymore.

"Tell me," I said again. "Please." Knowing what he wanted might give me an idea of what kind of spirit it was, which would lead, I hoped, to a way to get rid of it. A young, angry boy we could handle. It was the supernatural that was fucking everything up.

"You want the truth?" he asked, his head cocking to the side like a bird's. "Come with me."

Oh, sure. That was going to happen.

"You hit me in the head," I pointed out. "Why should I trust you?"

"You were sent away?" he asked. "When you did not become Crow."

It was almost more a statement than a question. It worried me but I shoved away the nagging feeling that something was weird about that. Everything was weird, what was one more bit to chew over later going to hurt?

"Yes," I said. "I was sent away, told to never come back. Kicked out of my own home. They said I was dead to them." I let some of my own anger and resentment show. *Building rapport. Goren and Eames would be proud.*

"You were lucky," he said. "I will show you the truth. Follow."

"Give me back my necklace," I said.

Without hesitation, he pulled the chain out from under his tunic and tossed my talisman to me. It glittered in the odd flickering blue light and I managed to catch it. Damn but it felt good to have the heavy silver D20 settle into place against my skin. I summoned my magic for a second, letting it flow through me and my talisman. Everything felt normal.

"Now you follow," he said.

I cast a glance back toward the cabins and Alek's trailer. I couldn't see it from here, the trees and darkness enfolding me, but I knew what Alek would say about taking this kind of risk. In my mind I saw Redtail's body, his chest ripped open, his ribs protruding. If taking this risk meant stopping that from happening again, it was worth it. No one else was going to die.

Except maybe Not Afraid.

I turned back to him, keeping hold of a thread of my magic so I had it easily available, and nodded for him to lead the way. Then I stepped beyond the boundary stone.

Moving through woods in daylight was enough of a pain in the ass. Walking through them at night was just plain crazy. I'd been working on some spells to augment myself during my training with Alek and my gaming buddies. One of those spells was darkvision. It didn't work quite the way I had hoped, at least not yet, and it wasn't easy to maintain, but I didn't want to cast a light until we were further away from the camp.

Ideally, the spell would have enabled me to see like it was daylight, only in black and white. The reality was more like an odd amber glow limning objects near me, making solid things shadowed and dark while their edges shimmered. It was good enough for me to follow Not Afraid without falling on my face or running into trees, but not much use beyond that. I couldn't move quickly, but Not Afraid patiently waited every time I stumbled or had to disentangle myself from a blackberry vine or dead branch.

He moved confidently through the woods, not making a sound. I couldn't tell if that was because he was just that good or if something seriously supernatural was going on. It had occurred to me that he might be a ghost, but then he would have been bound by the same general rules as a spirit and unable to affect the physical world this much without serious help from someone corporeal. I noticed that ferns and brush moved as he passed. So he had some solidity. I mentally checked off the box labeled "preternaturally quiet" and left it at that.

I couldn't tell what direction we were going. Only faint patches of stars glinted through the thick tree branches and I didn't spare much time for staring upward. With my darkvision running, light wasn't a pleasant thing to look at. Even the flickering blue in Not Afraid's eyes was disorienting any time I met his gaze as he waited for me to catch up.

After what felt like hours, I heard running water. A few minutes later, I could smell the stream and the air shifted to feeling more open. The forest fell away in an abrupt line and a wide, rocky ravine spread out below me. My vision wouldn't let me see too deeply into it, but amber light limned a field of boulders. To my right loomed a huge cliff, the top lost to the clash between the slowly brightening sky and my night vision.

The sky was turning from black to the dull grey of false dawn. It was enough that my normal vision could start to pick out details, I thought, so I dropped the night vision. I kept a hold on my magic, not trusting my companion or the spirit not to fuck with me.

The cliff rose a good hundred feet up from the floor of the ravine, the top outlined against the grey sky. The heavily sloping field was mostly rockfall but overgrown, as though the rocks had tumbled down a long time ago and nature was filling in the cracks. Boulders dotted the terrain like the bodies of sleeping beasts half covered in dew-speckled grass blankets. Down the hill to my left cut a creek, its cheery burble at odds with the mostly silent morning. Even the birds weren't speaking.

The rocky field had the same eerie stillness I associate with graveyards, and it unnerved me. Places can have their own power, their own energy. Sometimes from ley lines and other earthly sources of power. Sometimes from events like earth quakes or eruptions. Sometimes from people, though it would be rare for a wilderness spot like this to take on power from humans. I had a sense that we were close to whatever Not Afraid wanted to show me.

Wolf materialized beside me and growled, her hackles up, her eyes fixed on the cliff. She didn't appear to like this place any better than I.

"What is it?" I whispered to her. She looked at me with her starry-night eyes and growled again. I took a step forward, moving out of the trees, but she stayed put, swinging her head from side to side, her growl fading into a whine.

"Fine," I muttered. "Stay here then."

Not Afraid let me take in the surroundings, ignoring that I was apparently talking to myself, and then started picking his way across the rocks toward the cliff face. I followed, looking around me warily as the shadows deepened and the sky grew lighter.

Not Afraid reached the base of the cliff and waited for me there. I clambered up beside him to where it leveled out somewhat. The cliff face itself was pitted and gouged by the elements, too steep for vegetation to take hold. White streaks ran down the rocks like tears and something about the place made me shiver as I stared upward.

The bottom of the cliff was missing. Time and water had hollowed out the base into a low cave deep enough I couldn't see to the back, though something deep within seemed to move. I refused to peer too closely. I had had enough of dark places for a long while after the mine.

Stalactites hung from the roof at the mouth of the cave, giving it the appearance of a gaping mouth waiting to crunch down. The area in front of the mouth had been dug away into a rough pit. The pit was still in shadow but there seemed to be bare branches stacked in it.

I gripped my D20 and called up light, sending it like a flare over the pit.

Not branches. Bones. Hundreds of bones in piles with more poking out from the earth beneath. The skulls were obviously human and I counted a dozen before I made myself stop.

"What is this place," I whispered. It felt wrong to speak loudly in the face of so much death. Perhaps this was just a burial site? I doubted it. The graveyard where the People buried their dead was back behind the big house and I knew there were graves there that were hundreds of years old, so this wasn't some ancient site for the Three Feathers tribe.

"This is where the fledglings who don't turn into crow go to die." Not Afraid came up beside me, his eyes fixed on the grim piles only a few feet below us. "Blood Mother and I are trying to find which bones are whose, but it is not easy. Most of the spirits here do not want to talk to us."

"Blood Mother?" I looked sideways at him. He was close enough I should have been able to feel heat coming off his skin, to smell his sweat. I might as well have been standing here alone.

"She is with me," he said. "She will be avenged."

He was talking about the spirit, I realized. A spirit of vengeance.

"Buttercup?" I guessed.

"She died here," he said, biting off the words like they hurt to say aloud. "I have only Blood Mother now."

"Did you kill these people?" I said, letting the identity of the spirit go for the moment.

He laughed, and the chill in my bones grew stronger.

"She does not see!" he cried, throwing his arms wide. His fingertips brushed my arm, cold but solid. "She will not believe, even here."

"Tell me," I said, turning to face him. "Tell me what this is."

I had a feeling already. I knew but didn't want to know.

"Sky Heart," he screamed at me and I felt his breath sting my cheek, cold and smelling of dust and death. Another sign he wasn't a ghost at least. "This is where he would bring them, the ones who did not change. The ones who changed but not into crow. He calls this 'the final flight.' But we call it the cliff of many tears."

"He throws them off the cliff," I said, taking a step back, unable to hold my ground in the face of so much rage and grief. "These are children."

I looked back at the pit; my light ball had died, forgotten by me in my horror, but the rising sun now cast light now into it, enough light that I could make out the bones for what they were.

"If they did not change and fly, they died. If they did not die, because they were other than crow, he would come down and finish them. This is why I hunt the People. Eventually the coward Sky Heart will have to face me. This time he will die."

"But I was only exiled. I wasn't killed. Is this still going on?" I hadn't been thrown off a cliff. Not that it would have killed me, nor would any other means aside from having my heart eaten by another sorcerer. Perhaps Sky Heart knew that, knew somehow that he couldn't kill me.

"Do the others know?" I thought of my mother, of her confusion over what was happening, over why Not Afraid had killed Sky Heart's wife a century ago. Over her insistence, decades earlier, that Jasper be the one to drive me away from the ranch, that he make sure the new family picked me up.

"It does not matter," he said. "They let it happen. They must pay."

"It matters to me," I said, though even as I did I questioned why I was trying to split hairs, to assign guilt. How does one process murder on this scale? Sky Heart, if what Not Afraid was telling me was true, was a serial killer. But Not Afraid had plenty of blood on his hands.

He'd let the fledglings live. Let Carlos live. Gone out of his way to make sure they were fed and unharmed.

Heartless killer with a drama streak out for vengeance. I had to keep that in mind. As well as the spirit, this Blood Mother. She had proven tricky, full of illusions in the forest.

I shook my head. "I cannot let you keep killing," I said. "Somehow this has to end."

Cold blue light flared in Not Afraid's eyes but he shrieked and violently shook his head.

"Let me show her," he said. The light flickered and he reached for me.

"What are you doing?" I took another step back and nearly fell over a rock. I gathered power in my hands, ready to unleash a blast of force at him.

"Do not fight it, please," he said. "Let us show you what happened."

Universe help me, I let go of my magic and he took my hands in his icy cold fingers. A wave of power rushed up through me.

For a moment I was two people, myself standing at the base of the cliff, clinging to a man who should be dead, and also a girl in a blue gingham dress at the top of the cliff, my hair loose and whipping around my face.

Then the vision settled and I was just the girl. Buttercup.

"What are you doing?" She/I cried.

Sky Heart advanced on her/me. He was younger, stronger, his hair with its mane of feathers floating and flapping in the strong wind like wings. Shishishiel's power hugged him like a dark mantle and she/I cringed.

"You are not Crow," he said. "You have one last chance, fledgling. This is your final flight."

"Please, please, no," she/I begged him. Not Afraid had changed, he was crow. She would too, she was his twin, she needed more time. Even as she/I thought these things, we knew that there was nothing inside her, no power, no connection to an Other, an animal self.

Her/my only connection was to Not Afraid. He wasn't here, but he was coming, her distress calling to him across the miles of forest.

Too late. Sky Heart lunged forward and grabbed her/my arms with bruising force. "Fly," he yelled, his breath hot on her/my tearstained cheeks.

Then she/me flew, thrown off the cliff. One moment there was dirt beneath her/my bare feet, the next just sky.

The clouds were steel above, unbroken, the sun hiding its face.

"Brother," she/me screamed as the flying turned to falling.

I jerked away from Not Afraid just as I felt the horrible crushing pain of impact, pulling myself back to the present, back to life. I staggered, going to my knees, tears running down my face as his grief stayed with me, flooding my own senses. He had felt her die; her memories lived on in him. She might not have been shifter, but she was born a twin to one, born with inhuman blood in her veins no matter how human she appeared. Buttercup lived on in Not Afraid, lived on as Blood Mother. I was sure of it now.

"I found her in the cave," Not Afraid murmured. He knelt down in front of me, his hands splayed in supplication. "That is where Sky Heart left them. He stripped her body, leaving her for animals to find and scatter the bones."

The vision was over, but I still saw her broken shape, now naked and twisted, covered in blood and dirt, discarded like trash on the cave floor.

"How many?" I asked. "How long?"

"I have found sixty skulls," he answered. "I started before; this is when I built the grave here in front. I tried to bury them, to quiet their spirits. That is when Blood

Mother found me. There is only one way to quiet the dead. Justice, vengeance."

"So you confronted Sky Heart, but he killed you." I didn't wait for him to nod before continuing. The pieces were falling into place. "How did you come back?"

"Some things are too important for death to stop. Blood Mother needed to regain her strength. And now Shishishiel has abandoned the People. Now was the time." The blue light was back in his eyes, casting shadows on his gaunt face.

"If Sky Heart dies, justice will have been done. No one else will need to die." I forced myself to meet those cold eyes.

"If they knew," he said.

"If." I cut him off. "That is a big if. I saw no one but Sky Heart in your sister's memory."

"I will kill them all if it means getting to Sky Heart."

I believed that. "You said Shishishiel has abandoned him. Why can't you get to him now?"

"There is still power in the stones, and Sky Heart carries a talisman. Like yours, but it keeps Blood Mother away. Without her help, I cannot kill him."

Looking at his face, seeing the intensity there, the desperate need, I knew why he had risked bringing me here, why he had showed me the vision and the bones.

"You want me to let you in," I said.

"You have power." He reached toward my D20 talisman and I flinched back. No way was he getting his hands on that again. "Our needs are not so different. You want to stop the killings; I want to kill only Sky Heart. He is the end." His expression grew more sly, and it was so adolescent and obvious I almost laughed.

Laughing would have been pretty bad, so I held it in. Teen boys do not like being laughed at and I doubted it would be any different with resurrected teen boys filled with the enraged spirit of their dead twin sister.

I leaned back on my heels, looking out over the ravine, looking away from the bones. He wanted to kill Sky Heart and he wanted my help. I wasn't sure how to feel about that. I did not like Sky Heart, and that dislike was quickly turning to hatred in the aftermath of the vision. It was hard to deny the evidence that my grandfather was a coldblooded killer as well as a narcissistic cult leader. I had suspected that he had killed Ruby, my grandmother, but it wasn't talked about and there had never been any evidence of it.

It would be simple to destroy the boundary, I thought. Magic like that worked as long as the anchors were sound. Destroy a boundary stone, and the magic should snap. Sky Heart's talisman would be harder to get, but the danger of an object like that was once it was removed, it no longer protected the person. If I could get it away from him, keep him from fleeing in his crow form. That was a lot of ifs.

But Blood Mother, the spirit, had proven very tricky with her illusions in the forest the day before. She had tried to fuck with my emotions. I didn't trust the spirit and that meant I couldn't trust Not Afraid. The vision felt so real, the bones were real, and this place had the energy of sorrow and evil about it. All that I could accept. Perhaps.

"I will help you," I said, meeting his cold gaze again. "But there are conditions."

"What conditions?" he asked. His mouth pressed into a thin line and I guessed from the flicker and dance of blue fire in his eyes that neither he nor Blood Mother liked the idea of strings attached.

Well, bully for them. They wanted my help, they could suck it up and do it my way.

"I will speak with Sky Heart first. He will tell me the truth and when I have verified what you say about him is true, then and only then will I break the wards and let you in. And only if you give your oath, on the bones and memory of Buttercup, that no one else will be harmed, that Sky Heart's death will end this and you will rest in peace."

He considered that for longer than I liked, but perhaps him thinking it over was a good thing. Agreeing too quickly would have been suspect.

"How will you make him tell the truth?" he said finally.

"I have a spell for that," I lied. It wasn't really a permanent lie. I had a few hours of walking back to the camp to figure out how I was going to cast a truth spell. I had some ideas.

"We agree," he said. "We give our oath. Killing Sky Heart will end our vengeance and justice will be done."

I searched his face for signs of a lie, but found none. He had given an oath. In my heart it felt right. I wanted to trust him, and an oath given from a spirit like this was serious. Breaking oaths for supernaturals like ourselves wasn't something done lightly. That would have to be enough.

Now I just had to figure out how to deal with Alek and Carlos. I doubted they were going to let me walk into camp, magically bind and interrogate Sky Heart, and then possibly let a murder happen.

As if reading my mind, Not Afraid spoke, "The lion and tiger have crossed the boundary. They hunt for you."

Them being out of camp would make things easier. If they didn't find me.

"Can you lead them away? Keep them busy until I can get back?" I asked. "Without hurting them," I added.

"Yes." Not Afraid flashed me a smile and for a moment looked as young as he had been when he died the first time. "I am good at being the deer."

"All right," I said. "You'll have to point me in the right direction to get back." I was going to do this. The killing had to end. As Not Afraid had said, justice needed doing, and it looked like it was up to me to see it done.

With grim thoughts and dangerous plans swirling through my head, I got to my feet and followed Not Afraid back into the woods.

9

I wasn't as far from the ranch as I'd thought. The darkness had made the going very slow and it took me less time to return. The sun rose, cresting the trees, and I judged something like two or three hours had passed by the time I encountered the boundary stone I'd passed on my way out.

It was enough time for cold certainty to fight off my doubts. Enough time for me to come up with the basics of a plan. Three months before, a warlock had tried to turn some of my friends into living batteries. He'd been able to incapacitate shifters and trap them in their animal bodies. I had stopped him and eaten his heart, taking his power so I could free my friends.

I didn't like going into Bernie's memories, tapping into his knowledge. He hadn't been a very sane or very nice man. I felt like it should have bothered me more to kill him, but every time I touched his power or accessed his knowledge I remembered why I wasn't bothered at all.

I stopped at the stone and placed a small rock I'd picked up in the woods an hour before on top of it. I had filled the pebble with my power until I felt it wouldn't hold more without blowing apart. Which it would, as soon as I told it to, in a blast designed to at least score if not break the boundary stone. The explosion would disrupt the ward.

If Sky Heart was guilty. I was sure he was, my mind going over and over the things Not Afraid had shown me and going over my own gut feelings about this place, about my grandfather.

But I would do what was right. I would cast my version of a circle of truth and I would hear his guilt from his own lips. I was sure this was the only way I could live with myself later. The murders had to stop but justice needed to be done, as well.

I looked around the gravel circle and saw a few people gathered in a group near one of the cabins, talking. The doors of one of the pole barns was wide open and there were sounds of people using tools inside. Further on I saw two women throwing pottery on wheels under the awning of another barn. The scene was more normal than it had been, domestic even.

As I stepped into the camp and walked toward the big house, I wished for a fleeting moment that Alek wasn't off on a wild goose chase. I wanted to ask him what he thought, tell him about what I had discovered. I hesitated at the steps of the house. I was acting alone again, the way I was used to doing things. My whole life since Samir had killed my true family, the family of my heart, I'd been alone. I wasn't used to having friends who I could trust with difficult things, friends who could handle themselves in the magical world. The real world.

Alek wasn't here. I shook my head. This was my choice. My decision. I would learn the truth and I would stop these murders. Alek would understand that.

My thoughts felt like lies and I shoved them away. If he saw the bones. If he knew.

The door opened and Sky Heart stepped out onto the porch, taking away my last moments to think.

"You will leave," he said, leveling the shotgun at me. "Now."

No more hesitation. I caught the gun with my magic and yanked, ripping it free from his hands to clatter uselessly onto the boards. Then I pushed my magic into a circle using the knowledge I'd gained from the late Bernie the warlock. The power formed a ward, locking Sky

Heart inside. I layered on a second spell courtesy of Bernie, a spell to keep him from reaching out to that other plane, from calling on his crow half and shifting.

What would have taken Bernie multiple items carefully researched and gathered and the power of a full moon and hours of ritual took me a couple of seconds.

Now for the coup de grace. Or as Harper would call it, the cup-dee-gracie.

I layered one more spell, forming my magic into a glowing white circle, envisioning the purity of truth, a light that pushed away all lies, all shadows, a light that would let nothing hide within it.

My head started to pound and I knew I wouldn't be able to hold the spells for long. Time for a chat with grandfather.

"Did you throw Not Afraid's sister off a cliff?" I asked, keeping the question as unambiguous as I could.

Sky Heart's mouth worked as he stood frozen inside my circles and his eyes blazed with rage.

"Yes," he said, the words hissing out of his throat.

Was that enough? No. I wanted to know more. I wanted to hear him admit to all of it.

"How many children have you thrown off that cliff?" I said, my voice rising. Behind me I heard people moving, coming closer. Good, I thought. Let them come. Let them hear.

"Jade?" Pearl called out to me, but I ignored her.

"Tell me," I said. "Tell them, Sky Heart. Tell them all how you killed their children."

"You don't understand. You are exile. You are not one of us. You should be dead. I should have killed you when you were a baby. I let your mother keep you. I was weak and now we are all punished for it." The hatred in his face shocked me and I almost lost the spells.

"How many?" I demanded. "Tell them."

"I do not know," he screamed. "All of them. All the ones who are not my people. They were abominations, insults to the pure blood of Shishishiel. Like you. Just like you."

I reached out with a thread of power and found my exploding stone. A slight nudge of more power and it went off. A crack reverberated through the camp.

"No! What have you done," Sky Heart shrieked.

I sprang forward, clearing the steps in a leap and broke my own circles by diving into them. I ripped the beaded bag from his neck, pulling him forward. I kicked his legs out from under him and jumped aside as he tumbled down the steps.

He sprang to his feet quicker than I expected and turned on me, snarling.

A huge crow dropped out of the clear sky like a comet of death, slamming into Sky Heart and carrying him back to the ground in a swirling cloud of feathers. He screamed as the crow's unnaturally curved and sharp talons dug into his chest. Blue-white fire ripped into Sky Heart, flowing from the crow's open beak.

He died screaming, his chest bursting open, as the crow ripped out his heart and turned it to ashes before my eyes.

I stood on the porch, the beaded bag in my hand, shaking as the adrenaline dump hit me in the aftermath of using so much power.

The crow, which I guessed was Not Afraid, looked up at me and cawed, his huge black wings spread.

"It is done," I said. "Justice is done."

"No." Jasper was the first to reach Sky Heart's body. He waved his arms at the giant crow as though he could shoo it away. "NO!" he cried again.

The crow looked at me and something in its gaze warned me, but not soon enough.

Not Afraid beat his wings and flew up into Jasper's face, his talons hooking into my father's chest. Blue fire spilled around them and Jasper screamed in pain.

I gathered my magic but couldn't blast the crow without hitting Jasper. I jumped off the porch and attacked the crow with my hands, tearing at his feathers. Cold burned me, icy fire rippling up my arms. More on instinct than with clear thought, I thrust the beaded talisman around Not Afraid's neck.

The Crow shrieked and shifted. Now I wrestled with Not Afraid himself. He looked fifteen but his body had a strength I couldn't match. Jasper went down and Not Afraid shoved me off, then came after me, ripping the talisman bag from his neck. He was free of my father. Free and clear for me to blast the shit out of him.

I summoned my power and sent a bolt of pure force at him. It should have ripped him apart, but he merely staggered and then laughed. His hands and face were covered in blood. My father's blood or Sky Heart's, I wasn't sure. It didn't matter.

"You broke your oath," I said as I struggled to my feet.

"I had a prior oath." He grinned at me, his gaunt and bloody face a death mask. He reached into his shirt and pulled out a small rectangular piece of paper, tossing it onto the ground.

I ignored it and lunged for him, sending another bolt of power at his face. His eyes flared blue and he shifted to a giant crow again even as he leapt to meet me.

Wolf sprang between us, her huge body slamming into the crow and knocking it aside. I twisted and managed to avoid colliding with her as well. She spun and snarled, spit dripping from razor-sharp teeth as long as my fingers.

Not Afraid beat his wings and lifted into the sky, circling once and then glowing with bright blue fire before disappearing into the sunlight like a ghost.

I let go of my magic, falling against Wolf's warm body as exhaustion hit me like a drunk driver with a lead foot. My foggy brain realized someone was crying, pleading over and over for someone not to leave them.

Jasper. I opened my eyes.

He lay in a spreading pool of blood, his chest ripped open, his heart a smoking ruin within a mess of pink lung tissue and too-bright red blood. I knew he was dead. Even a shifter can't heal a vital organ destroyed by fire.

Pearl knelt over him, his head in her lap, smoothing her hands over his hair again and again, her pleading a high keening, the words blending and melding until they meant nothing. Emerald stood behind Pearl, her face pale with shock, her green eyes wide and unseeing. As I watched, shudders and shakes took over her body and she dropped to her knees and clung to her mother.

Movement to my side caught my eye as something fluttered on the ground. The paper that Not Afraid had removed from his shirt.

Slowly, as though I had aged a thousand years, I staggered over and picked it up.

It was a post card.

I crumpled the post card in my hand, igniting it with a thought as I let it flutter toward the ground again. It was ash even as it hit.

A scream that shifted to a high-pitched snarl was my only warning. Em rose to her feet and sprang at me, shifting in midair into a white wolf. I threw my hands up and pushed magic out into a shield in front of me.

She bounced off the shield and twisted, landing on her feet. She sprang again and again I forced her away.

"Em," I yelled. "I don't want to hurt you."

Snarl. Leap. Bounce. Twist. Repeat.

Then people around us started shifting, turning into crows. They rose as a black swarm into the sky and descended at me, dive-bombing me like I was a bird of prey.

I pulled my power around me like a dome and hunkered down, throwing everything I had into keeping the shield up. Through the barrage of black wings I caught Pearl watching, Jasper's head still in her lap, and I silently pleaded with her to stop this, to call them off.

She shook her head and looked away from me, her face quickly lost in the slam and flurry of winged bodies.

I couldn't hold the shield forever. They wouldn't be able to kill me, but I had no idea what happened to a sorceress who is torn apart. How long would it take to regenerate? Years? What would that pain feel like? Would I be conscious?

Em's wolf body slammed into my shield again and this time I felt the reverberation right down into my bones. I was going to lose it soon, there was too much physical force being thrown against me.

The deep coughing roar of a lion echoed through the camp and suddenly the crows all came to earth, changing as they touched down back into their human forms. Em hit my shield one last time and rebounded, turning even as she twisted in the air back to a teenage girl.

A huge white tiger leapt between Em and I. Alek. I dropped my shield and called out his name.

He shifted to human and looked around, taking in the two mutilated corpses and the cluster of angry shifters. Carlos, still in his lion form, prowled through the People, cutting a line between them and where Alek and I stood.

"What happened here?" Alek said. His voice was deceptively soft, but carried some of the tiger's growl still in it, a dangerous tone.

"She broke the wards," Pearl said, pointing at me. "She allowed the evil in."

"That's not the whole story," I protested. "Sky Heart has been killing the fledglings who don't turn into crow. He murdered dozens of them. I have seen their bones. He admitted as much to me, to all of us, before Not Afraid killed him."

Alek turned and looked at me, disbelief and a deep sadness in his eyes.

"You let him in?"

"Yes," I said. I spread my hands, half reaching for Alek as I stared up at him, begging him to believe my good intentions. "We made a deal. He could get his justice, then he would rest and the People would be left in peace. He gave me his oath."

"He broke an oath?" Alek looked like he wanted to understand, but he stayed where he was, and I dropped my hands.

"He had a prior oath." I couldn't share my suspicions about Samir's involvement, not here in front of everyone. "He betrayed me and killed Jasper."

"You stupid girl," Pearl said. She rose to her feet after gently setting Jasper's head on the ground. "Not Afraid is an evil spirit. That is no boy. I saw him die more than a century ago. Whatever that is, it cannot be him."

"You heard Sky Heart," I said. "You heard him. He killed those children. Why do you think Shishishiel has abandoned you? Why did the great Crow not stop this?"

I knew it was unfair to invoke their missing guardian, but I had been trying to help them. They couldn't see that. They could only see the dead bodies. They hadn't seen the bones. Hadn't seen how many more deaths I was trying to prevent.

Gasps and questions from the crowd turned quickly to angry murmurs and Carlos roared again, quieting them. I stood up, every muscle protesting and my head pounding like it was going to explode.

"Go," Pearl screeched at me. "Go from here, killer. We will take care of our own, as we always have."

Alek reached for me then, his hand closing on my upper arm as he stepped in close. "Get in the truck," he murmured. "I will get you out of here in one piece if I can."

I looked past him, forcing myself to see Jasper's body. For fourteen years he had been my father. For more than thirty after that, he had been as good as dead to me. Then I had learned he wasn't even my birth father.

But he had come to me for help. Not Alek, not the Council of Nine. Me. He'd been so desperate, but also trusting that somehow I could come here and make things better.

I had failed him. I had seen only what I wanted to see, believed what I wanted to believe. He had paid the price for it. He was the one walking along the road to hell my good intentions had paved.

"No," I said, blinking away tears. I had no right to grieve for this man. But I did have the duty to set things right, to fulfill the promise I'd made him by coming here. Samir was somehow at the root of this, I could feel it. My guess was he had raised Not Afraid from the dead, reuniting him with Blood Mother and setting them loose on my family.

"No," I repeated, pulling my arm out of Alek's grip. "I am going to kill Not Afraid and lay Buttercup's spirit to rest once and for all. No one else dies."

"You do not have that right," Pearl said.

"I have every right. Jasper begged me to come and I promised I would help. I am going to end this. I will not break my word." I started walking, glaring at the crowd, daring them to get in my way.

"Wait," Alek said, coming up beside me. "We will come with you."

"What if he comes back here?" I said. "Who will protect them?"

I didn't think Not Afraid would come here. I was pretty damn sure where he had flown off to. But Alek couldn't come with me. This was my fight and I didn't know if I could protect him, too. Or even if I could win. I didn't want to worry about him.

And there really was a small chance that Not Afraid would double back, counting on me to try to follow him and instead coming to finish killing the People.

"Carlos," Alek said. "He'll stay."

"Because he was so effective against this guy before?" I hated the mean whine in my voice, but I had to convince Alek to stay out of my way.

Carlos snarled at me.

"Fuck you," Alek said. I was pushing him away, as obviously as the physical distance opening between us. I wanted his anger. I needed him to stay here. Stay safe, away from me.

"Please," I whispered, turning to Alek. "Please protect them. Don't let anyone else die."

It was underhanded and totally manipulative and I felt terrible pulling the trick, but it worked. There was enough truth in my pleading, in my grief, that he fell for it. That or he gave up on me. I didn't want to know.

"Fine." The finality in his tone was like charging into a wall.

"Wolf," I called and this time she appeared. She seemed to recognize what I wanted and bent low so I could drag myself up onto her back. There was no way in nine hells I was getting back to the cave without help. My body was exhausted, my magic a weak throb inside of me. I hoped I could find a second wind somewhere on the run there.

Wolf and I plunged through the crowd and no one made a move to stop us. Soon the cool forest canopy closed over us. I clung to Wolf's fur and tried to think about how in the power of the Universe I was going to kill a man who was already dead.

The rocks in the ravine looked like poorly cut gravestones jabbing through the inconsistent moss and grass clinging perilously to their edges. The cliff loomed, the tears streaking its face glinting in the sunlight. It cast a shadow over its base, as though deliberately hiding the pit of bones there.

Wolf stopped at the treeline again and I slid off her back. My legs felt like rubberbands and my head still ached, but I was more rested than I would have been if I'd run here under my own power. I was grateful that Wolf was with me.

Back to normal, she and I against Samir. Or in this case, one of Samir's stupid plots.

Not that stupid, a treacherous voice inside me whined, *you fell for it. This is what you get for not running when you had the chance.*

"It ain't over yet," I said aloud.

Wolf and I picked our way across the ravine to the cave. I had hoped that Not Afraid would be outside, though fighting him in the open would give him the advantage of flight. Wolf had managed to rebuff him when he was in his crow form. Carlos had said that he didn't think the boy was a shifter. I figured that he had lost that power when he died and was brought back. The diabolical crow form was probably Blood Mother giving him her power, which meant that in that form, Wolf could hurt him.

Rustling in the rear of the cave caught my attention. I crept around the pit and stopped at the entrance. I didn't want to go back into the dark, back beneath tons of earth and stone. I summoned my magic, debating just spamming bolts of pure power throughout the damn cave to see if I could flush Not Afraid out.

Great. My plan was apparently to Magic Missile the darkness. There had to be a better way.

"Not Afraid," I called out. "Come face me, you bastard."

Silence. Then rustling and hissing. With my luck the cave was full of snakes or something. The hissing reminded me of the noise a crow makes when angry, however. Not a sibilant sound so much as air being forced out of a small throat.

I pooled power in my hands, willing it into a bright purple goo that phosphoresced. Then I flung the goo into the cave, throwing my hands wide so that it splattered across as wide an area as I could manage. The light goo painted the stalactites and the cave floor, revealing a wide cavern with a ceiling that would have forced Alek to duck along the outer edge but opened up toward the back. The glow illuminated enough that I could make out shapes. There was something at the back of the cave, a shape that clearly wasn't a stalactite or stalagmite.

With a deep breath and more power at the ready, I moved into the cave. I crept toward the rustling and movement from the shape at the back. As I neared, I formed another ball of light goo and spattered the stalactites above me with it.

The shape resolved itself into a cage of human bones. Inside the cage was a giant crow that looked like something out of a Resident Evil movie. Its feathers were caked with ichor and dried blood, with large patches sloughed off and other hanging by threads of flesh. Its mouth was open, making that horrid hissing noise I'd heard before. The crow looked at me as Wolf started growling again.

Its eyes were exactly like Wolf's eyes. Full black with pinpricks of light like a backcountry sky on a moonless night.

Undying. The ancient guardians of the beings who became the human's gods.

Shishishiel.

He hadn't abandoned the People. He was trapped. Tortured and somehow decaying.

Wolf's fur isn't perfectly black anymore. Down her belly is a thick line of white scar tissue. A parting gift from Samir. We had barely made it away from him alive. He was the only person I knew who could hurt an Undying.

"Beautiful, isn't it?" Not Afraid slunk out from behind a stalagmite at the back of the cave. "Samir was very helpful. Now you see why I had to honor my oath to him? He promised me vengeance. He stopped Shishishiel."

Shishishiel shrieked and tried to open his wings, but the bone cage prevented it.

I unleashed my magic, slamming pure force into the cage, not daring to speak first lest I warn Not Afraid of my intentions. Nothing happened. It was as though the cage ate my magic. I grabbed it with my hands and was rebuffed by a shield of power that hovered just above the bones. The force of it threw me back and I slammed into a stalagmite. Crystalline rocks crashed about me and stung my face and arms as they fell.

This cave was fragile. Good to remember. I didn't fancy getting impaled.

"That will not work," Not Afraid said.

"What will?" I asked. I didn't expect him to answer, it was more to buy time for Wolf to circle around behind me and come up on his flank.

Not Afraid just laughed; his face again a death mask in the purple light of my spell. Blue fire danced in his eyes and limned his body. I prayed that meant the spirit was in him, which would mean Wolf could help. He drew a large knife from a sheath at his waist. I wondered if it had always been there but hidden by illusions, or if he had come back here to weapon up. I thought of Gibb's rule nine from *NCIS*. Always carry a knife.

Another thing I was going to change if I made it out of this situation.

"Where is Samir?" I slowly got to my feet, careful to make no move that might provoke an attack.

Not Afraid shrugged. "Not here. He said if you could not handle us, you would not be worth his time. He was not even sure you would come. But I was. I know the Crow. Blood calls to blood. No one leaves Sky Heart's Tribe alive."

Wolf sprang at Not Afraid and he twisted, slashing with the knife. The blade glowed with red fire, power I recognized.

"Wolf, no!" I yelled. Samir had enchanted that knife. It was too late. The blade cut into Wolf's shoulder and she howled, iridescent blood spurting from her wound. I threw a bolt of magic at Not Afraid. It was easily deflected by a burst of blue energy and fizzled before doing more than distracting him momentarily.

A moment was enough for Wolf to get away. She was the size of a pony and her ability to maneuver inside the cave was limited by the crystalline growths. She limped backward, snarling.

"You can't kill me," I said, taunting Not Afraid, trying to make him focus only on me. "Did Samir tell you that? He's setting you up. Fucking with you. This is all just one of his stupid games, a way to hurt me."

"There are worse fates than death," Not Afraid replied, turning to me. He wiped the blade on his leathers and grinned. "Just ask Shishishiel."

Shishishiel. Not Afraid was between me and the cage, but I could see the crow's pained eyes beyond us. As I watched, a droplet of milky water fell from an overhead stalactite and splashed onto the cage, running down the yellowed bones.

Shishishiel, my mind repeated. The crow spirit had stopped Not Afraid and Blood Mother a century before. He was dangerous enough that Samir had neutralized him before resurrecting Not Afraid. Free the crow, save the People.

It didn't have quite the same ring as "save the cheerleader, save the world," but I would work with the ideas I had.

The water got through. The crystals were fragile, but I was willing to bet a whole stalactite would be pretty heavy. Heavy enough to break bones?

"Is the cage made from your sister?" I asked, buying time as I gathered my magic again. I couldn't use gestures. Nothing could give away what I was planning or Not Afraid would attack. I had to keep him talking. In the end, he was just a kid. A totally crazy kid with the insane rage spirit echo of his dead twin sister living inside him. Still, he had talked to Carlos. He seemed to want someone to listen.

"Yes," he said, his eyes narrowing. "Why?"

"After you cut me up or whatever, are you going to kill the rest of the People?" I formed my magic into a razor-thin disk over my head, not daring to look up and check my work. I hoped Blood Mother couldn't see my magic. Not Afraid wasn't reacting so far, and as they say, so far, so good.

"I will wipe out the bloodlines." His lips curled back from his teeth.

"Even my sister? She isn't crow. She's just a kid, just like Buttercup."

"No," he said. "She isn't. She's of your blood, of Sky Heart's blood. They all must die. They all must suffer." He took a step toward me, brandishing the blade. "You will suffer first."

"You weren't going to keep your oath to me even if you hadn't cut a deal with Samir, were you?" I asked.

I didn't give him time to answer. I already knew what he would say. Envisioning the invisible weapon like Xena's chakram, I threw the magic disk at the stalactite above the cage.

The magic chakram sheered through the crystal. The stalactite crashed down, smashing into the bones.

Not Afraid screamed and attacked as the cage shattered. Bone and crystal fragments flew everywhere, pieces embedding themselves in my body with searing force. I threw myself sideways, my hands up to protect my face. Not Afraid came down on top of me and I grabbed at his arms, struggling to keep the knife away from my body. He straddled me, his superior strength winning out as the knife blade dug into my chest. Blue fire rippled around his arms and joined the red fire burning a hole into my breastbone.

The screaming was all me. I tried to fight the panic, fight the feeling that I was about to die. It is hard to remember you are immortal when your heart is slowly being burned out of your chest.

I wasn't even sure that Samir's knife couldn't kill me. I really didn't want to find out I'd been wrong all these years about how to kill a sorceress.

Wolf's jaws closed on Not Afraid's shoulder as she sprang at him and tried to drag him off me, her head whipping back and forth. I tried to gather power, to blast him off my chest, but the pain was too much. Red spots danced in my vision like blood spatter and cold darkness closed in, fogging my mind.

Then a woman appeared over Not Afraid. She was Native, her skin perfectly red-brown and smooth, her face ageless, young and ancient somehow all at once. Her eyes met mine and all I saw were stars as she reached for his head with strong, graceful hands.

She broke his neck.

Blue energy swirled up from him but the woman shook her head and opened her mouth. Blood Mother's power swirled in the air, seeming to resist for a moment like a child who doesn't want to go to bed yet. Then it flowed into her mouth and was gone.

She pulled Not Afraid off me and the knife clattered to the ground.

"Shishishiel," I whispered. I'd always thought of the Crow as a man. Sky Heart had always called the spirit "he." I guess we see what we want to see.

The woman turned away from me and touched Wolf's injured shoulder. The leak of iridescent blood stopped and the wound closed.

I realized then that Shishishiel wasn't Undying. She was one of the beings the Undying guarded.

She stared into Wolf's eyes for a long moment as though they were holding an intimate conversation. For all I knew, they were. Then she shifted to a crow shape and flew out of the cave, leaving only the faint murmur of wings behind her.

I used Wolf's leg to pull myself up and forced myself to look down at my chest. The bleeding had stopped but there was a ragged wound with charred edges, and it smelled like bacon.

"You got some 'splaining to do," I muttered at Wolf. Which was pointless. Wolf wouldn't tell me anything even if she could. I had a lot of sudden suspicions about how she came to protect me, however, all of which led to a lot more questions.

Questions I could ponder when I wasn't two breaths away from passing the fuck out. I picked up the magic knife. Instinct told me to destroy it, but logic told me to bring it with me. I couldn't leave it. The blade was too dangerous. Not Afraid had a sheath belted to his waist with a leather cord. I pulled it free of his corpse and slung it over my shoulder after putting away the blade.

With Wolf as my crutch, I stumbled my way out of the cave, blinking in the bright sunlight. One foot in front of another, we made our way across the ravine and back toward camp. Despite Shishishiel closing Wolf's wound, my guardian was still limping, and I wasn't sure I had the strength to stay on her back. So we walked. Or shambled. Shuffled. Stumbled. One foot in front of the other. Over and over.

I don't know how far I got. A mile? Less, probably. There were lots of trees still. And sword ferns which rose up to catch me as I slumped into them.

The next thing I knew, Alek was bending over me.

"Is it over?" he asked. Not, "Are you all right?" or another expression of concern. He didn't try to touch me, either. That worried me but I shoved it aside.

"Yes," I croaked. "He's dead."

It wasn't over, however. I had a feeling this was just Samir's opening salvo. His shot across my bow.

"Good," Alek said. Then his voice softened, and he added, "Rest, I've got you." He picked me up gently in his warm arms.

"We have to stop meeting like this," I said. Then red-tinged darkness roared up and pulled me under.

Either I had made it further than I thought or I stayed passed out for a lot longer than it felt like, because it seemed like barely any time had gone by before we emerged from the forest and into the camp.

The People were gathered again, standing in loose rows, filling the open space in front of the big house. Pearl stood over the two bodies. Both had been wrapped now with indigo burial sheets. No one said a word. They watched us pass in eerie silence as Alek carried me toward where his truck was parked. It appeared we were going to get the hell out of Dodge.

"Wait," I said, my throat still feeling like I'd swallowed gravel and my chest still on fire with every breath. "Put me down."

"I don't think that is a good idea," Alek said.

I started to struggle and he had no choice. I stumbled, grabbing his arm to steady myself. Wolf was nowhere in sight.

"You must go," Pearl said. She seemed less angry now, but there was a hard finality in her words that allowed no argument.

"What will happen to Em?" I asked, gesturing at the angry girl standing near Pearl. My half sister had shifted, but not into a crow. I wanted to believe that my mother wouldn't throw her off a cliff at least, but this was the same woman who had sent me away to live with an abusive couple.

I thought about what Sky Heart had said about wanting to kill me young. I thought about the bones beneath the cliff. Perhaps my mother had known, had suspected. She had tried to save me. I pushed that thought aside.

"Em is staying with us," Pearl said. "We must change to survive. Sky Heart's ways brought evil to the People. We will not send our children away. Never again."

"Send them away? He was killing them." I couldn't believe she was still talking around his crimes.

"Enough. What is done is done. This is not for you to know, not for you to be a part of anymore. We cannot forgive you, but for your atonement in killing Not

Afraid, we will allow you to leave." As she spoke, the shadow of wings unfurled at the corners of my vision and I knew that Shishishiel was with her. My mother, the new Sky Heart. I hoped she would be a gentler dictator.

"What about my father?" I asked. I didn't need to clarify I wasn't talking about Jasper.

"His secrets are not mine to reveal. If he wants you to know him, he will find you." She came toward me, the mantle of Shishishiel's power fading back, leaving only my mother's familiar form behind.

"I'm sorry," I whispered.

"Go," she said, but this time the words were a plea more than a command. "We must take care of our own."

I had no strength left to argue. Emerald would get to stay in her home. That was something at least. I wanted to warn Pearl about Samir, but realized that Shishishiel had likely already done so. There was nothing here for me.

"Goodbye, mother," I said.

I used Alek's sink to wipe the worst of the blood off my chest and changed my shirt. The wound was closed already, but I knew I wouldn't be eating delicious pork products with quite the same gusto for a long while. Black and purple bruising were already spreading over my whole chest, creating a nebulae pattern that would make Hubble fanatics jealous.

Then I climbed into the truck and Alek drove us away from Three Feathers. We were silent until we had made it well out of sight of the camp.

"Where is Carlos?" I asked to break the tension.

"They had hidden his car when he disappeared. He went to retrieve it after Pearl said that Not Afraid was dead. She said you were hurt. That was when I went to find you."

"Ah," I said. The long night, the longer day, and sheer exhaustion slammed into me. My father, the man I had thought was my father, was dead. Samir had tried to wipe out my entire bloodline.

I had almost played right into his hands. I had maybe almost died.

I had let a man be murdered. A terrible man, true, but his blood was as much on my hands as on Not Afraid's.

I started shaking and curled up in the seat, wrapping my arms around myself and taking quick, shallow breaths. Deep ones still hurt too much to manage. Fat tears leaked down my cheeks.

Alek looked over at me but said nothing.

"Aren't you going to ask if I'm okay," I stuttered through my tears, trying to crack a smile. I feared it looked more like a grimace.

"No," he said with a look that made it clear he knew I wasn't okay. A look that said we weren't okay.

We left it at that. I turned my head and stared out the window, watching the land go by in a green blur through my tears.

I had stopped Not Afraid and Blood Mother. I had even mostly thwarted Samir's plan to wipe out the People.

I didn't know the cost yet, not fully. I had only learned how little I really knew about my past and my heritage, about how the world really worked. This was a Pyrrhic victory, at best.

But one truth I did know was that there was no going back. Eventually the tears dried up and I faced forward. Toward the future. Toward home.

If you want to be notified when Annie Bellet's next novel or collection is released, please sign up for the mailing list by going to: http://tinyurl.com/anniebellet. Your email address will never be shared and you can unsubscribe at any time. Want to find more Twenty-Sided Sorceress books? Go here http://overactive.wordpress.com/twenty-sided-sorceress/ for links and more information.

Word-of-mouth and reviews are vital for any author to succeed. If you enjoyed the book, please tell your friends and consider leaving a review wherever you purchased it. Even a few lines sharing your thoughts on this story would be extremely helpful for other readers. Thank you!

Author's Note:

This book is wholly a work of fiction. However, I did borrow a little from the language and traditions of the Apsaalooké, or Crow, people who are alive and well today in the United States. Jade's Crow people are quite different and I took many fictional liberties, of course, but I wanted a foundation in reality since sometimes the best fantasy stems from the world we already know.

If you are interested in learning more about the actual Apsaalooké and the modern Crow Nation, please visit their website as a starting point:

http://www.crow-nsn.gov/

Also by Annie Bellet:

The Gryphonpike Chronicles:
Witch Hunt
Twice Drowned Dragon
A Stone's Throw
Dead of Knight
The Barrows (Omnibus Vol. 1)

Chwedl Duology:
A Heart in Sun and Shadow
The Raven King

Pyrrh Considerable Crimes Division Series:
Avarice

Short Story Collections:
The Spacer's Blade and Other Stories
River Daughter and Other Stories
Deep Black Beyond
Till Human Voices Wake Us
Dusk and Shiver
Forgotten Tigers and Other Stories

About the Author:

Annie Bellet lives and writes in the Pacific NW. She is the author of the *Gryphonpike Chronicles* and the *Twenty-Sided Sorceress* series, and her short stories have appeared in over two dozen magazines and anthologies. Follow her on her blog at "A Little Imagination".

http://overactive.wordpress.com/

CPSIA information can be obtained at www.ICGtesting.com
Printed in the USA
LVOW10s2257110515

438129LV00004B/226/P